It's Her Thickness for Me

Written By

Lady Lissa

&

Shelli Marie

Prologue

Cashay Taylor

Blocking the sun's strong rays with my forearm, I eased out of our apartment to hear a bunch of screaming and hollering. Insecure with my size behind the constant teasing made me hesitant to join the other kids until I caught my best friend Katrina's voice calling out to Demisha.

Taking my chances, I strolled cautiously over to where the girls were standing. "What y'all playin'?"

"Girl, something you don't wanna play!" Demisha answered like somebody was talking to her because I sure wasn't. "It's hot out here and you know you ain't about to run around no bases!"

"How you know?!" Katrice challenged with her hands on her hips.

"Because her big ass gonna be outta breath by the time she gets to first base!" she yelled and fell out laughing causing a domino effect.

As the other kids cracked up, the mean bitch Demisha continued to talk mess, but I didn't have nothing to say to her. My size shouldn't have mattered to her! It shouldn't have mattered to anybody and at ten years old, even I knew that shit!

"I don't see what's so damn funny!" Katrice barked hushing the laughter. "Let Cashay play! Or are y'all scared she might be better than y'all?"

"Scared she might run us over like a big mack truck, yea!" Demisha laughed loudly until Tay, Katrice's older cousin, stepped out and shut her damn pie hole for her.

"Let her play!" he hissed. "I can't believe y'all teasing this little girl. Especially you Demisha wit' yo messed up grill and knees as ashy as dirt!"

Everyone started laughing and it took everything in me for me to not bust out laughing too.

"FUCK YOU TAY!" she hollered on the verge of tears as she licked her nasty fingers and tried to rub the ash off her knees.

"Watch yo mouth before I go get yo mama!" he threatened before he left us out there to work things out ourselves.

"Whatever! Ain't nobody worried about him!" she mumbled under her breath, but Katrice heard her and so did I.

"You need to be worried before yo mama come out here and embarrass you!" Katrice scoffed and stood there with the ball. "Now who wants to play and who wants to just stand here? Because if you ain't playing, get out the way!"

Demisha and her little crew decided that they wanted to stay and good thing they did because when it was my turn to kick, it was on. Since this girl chose to be pitcher, soon as she released the ball onto the ground towards me, I swung my foot forward as hard as I could. Man! Those kids were so surprised when the ball went over the fence and so was I!

Actually, I was proud of myself until Demisha insisted that I went around the fence to get the ball myself. Ugh, I hated the girl! Talking about I needed the exercise anyway.

"I see that my kick didn't shut her up but the next time I get up there, I'm gonna let her have it!" I panted all out of breath as I walked all the bases first then went to get the ball and threw it over the fence and back onto the field.

"You okay Cashay?" Katrice checked and slapped me a high-five for my kick and score.

"Thank... thank... thank you!" I stuttered still trying to regulate my breathing.

It wasn't until 20 minutes later that I was feeling myself again. Just in time for my next kick.

"Oh, shit! Everyone stand back!" Demisha warned still pushing my buttons. If she didn't learn the last time, she would definitely take heed after what I had planned for her ass this time around.

As she rolled the ball to me, this time I aimed my foot directly at her so that when it reached me, I could kick it right on point. Yep! Right between those evil ass eyes!"

POW!

As the ball of thick rubber hit her dead in the face, she went flying backwards onto the ground. Everyone ran over to check on Demisha while I took my time walking the bases as the ball sat unattended in the middle of the field.

My foot touched home base just as she rose and started yelling at me. Usually, I would retreat to the house to avoid another confrontation but after seeing her humiliated not once, but twice, I wanted to hear what she had to say.

"Scored again!" I cheered while Demisha's girls held her back.

"You did that shit on purpose bitch!" she raged still trying to get at me.

"Did what?" I asked, as if I didn't already know what she was talking about.

"YOU HIT ME WITH THAT BALL ON PURPOSE!!" Demisha hollered like a damn fool as she continued to try to get at me. I was curious to see what she would do if her friends let her go, so I took a different approach than what I would normally take.

"Let her go! Ain't nobody about to run from her!" I sneered with my arms folded across my chest.

Her friends did just that and let her go. She turned to look at them with a questioning expression on her face. Shit, she was probably wondering why they let her go. As long as they held her back, she was talking that shit, but as soon as they let her go, she didn't even buck up!

Finally, I had intimidated Demisha and now she was the one running in the house. Just like I thought... she was nothing but a 'scary bully'! She talked a good game, but she wasn't ready at all.

Needless to say, that was the last time Demisha, and I got into it only because she stayed clear of me. That was fine by me. It wasn't like I was trying to be her buddy any darn way.

Katrice was enough of a friend for me, and I was good with that. Well, at least until I got older and started thinking about the opposite sex! Once that happened, I found myself with a bigger problem than Demisha... BOYS!

After I became interested in guys, I felt insecure all over again! Ugh! Now I had a whole other issue to get over...

Lord, please allow me to love the skin I'm in like I used to! Please, Lord, Please...

Chapter One

Fifteen Years Later...

Cashay Taylor

Proudly smiling at my reflection in the mirror with my best friend standing beside me, I thought about how far both me and Katrice had come. When we met at ten, we clicked right away. Then when her mother died three years later, she had come to live with us. My mama raised her like she was her own making Katrice the sister that I never had. We may not have had a father in our lives, but my mama did it all!

My mother, Gena, was the epitome of the perfect mom! She worked, cooked, cleaned and spent plenty of time with us. She even put us through community college and made sure that we had a car to get there to obtain our degrees! While Katrice chose to go into the accounting field, I followed my heart and became a teacher.

With our lives flourishing, we moved out of moms' and rented a small, one-level, three-bedroom home that was located in North Houston. Not only was the rent cheaper, but it was also more of a diverse neighborhood. There was a little bit of everybody around here. From tall to short, dark to light, fat to skinny, and hustlers to hard workers.

It took a minute, but I was slowly starting to feel like I fit in. The more I ate right and took my daily walks, the more confidence I was building. Now, I was even taking chances that I wouldn't have normally taken. Like this outfit that I was trying to rock to the club tonight.

"I'm wearing this tonight Cashay!" Katrice bragged as she held up the cutest skirt and hoodie set with the wedged sneakers to match.

It was some new line Adidas that was too out of the norm for me. Now Katrice, she could rock the shit out of it and anything else for that matter. With a body like a runway model, she had it going on and that was just why she had been my inspiration over the past 10 years.

"I don't know about this one boo," I told Katrina who stared me down with a head shake.

"I voiced my opinion when you first ordered it. Personally, I think it looks good, but it's all on you Cashay!!" she argued. "You know what you like and what you're comfortable in."

Boy oh boy, I should've listened to my best friend Katrice when she told me to be cautious about the crop top, jogger set that I saw on Amazon. For a XXXL it was only nine dollars! Who could pass that up? Not me! I loved a good bargain!

"You think it looks okay?" I asked her before we left out the door to the club.

"Cashay, if you feel comfortable in it, you're your head up high and sport that muthafucka with confidence! But if you're gonna cry soon as somebody calls you fat..."

"You think I look fat in this?" I asked looking at the pudge around my midsection. It had gone down quite a bit, but it was still visible.

"Hips, ass, tits, thighs... you're a big girl and you know it Cashay. Why are you asking me some shit like that?"

Just the mention of the word 'fat' had rubbed me the wrong way since I was a kid. All the mean rugrats from school and the neighborhood would tease me all the time about my weight and height, but to me it was normal. Everyone in my family was tall and thick.

"You right girl!" I laughed as I stared at myself in the mirror and embraced my outer beauty. "I am big! Thick if you may!"

"You crazy Cashay! But you good?"

"I'm good! Let's go!" I spoke boldly as I checked my lashes, gloss, and flipped my hair before prying myself from my reflection so that we could leave out the door. Hopping in the car, I clicked my seatbelt and checked the mirrors.

"Damn!" I screamed.

The volume on the radio was super high when I keyed the ignition. It blasted so loud that it shook the whole car and scared the shit out of me in the process. The way I nearly jumped out my skin while reaching for anything that could brace me, had Katrice cracking up.

"That shit ain't funny!" I smirked then laughed and shook my head as I pulled off from the house.

While I drove down to the Red Rooster on Almeda, Katrice bobbed her head and danced in her seat. Bouncing her body to the beat, she flowed flawlessly with Nicki Minaj as she rapped on some new single that was playing on satellite radio.

"Damn! We got here fast!" Katrice cheered bringing me from the daze that boosted my confidence as I parked, got out and walked in the club with my head held high. That shit lasted all of ten minutes.

"Y'all see this big bitch?!" Anita hollered out gaining everybody's attention.

This bitch Anita wasn't nothing but a darker version of Demisha from my childhood. The way she tried to clown me brought back all the painful memories and I couldn't stop myself from unleashing the beast on her ass just to teach her a lesson.

Downing my drink, I slammed my glass onto the bar and waited for the bitch to say another word. It didn't take but a few seconds.

"Just because they make it in your size, don't mean you should wear it! You don't even have the body type for that shit! She probably ordered that shit off Amazon even though it looks like some shit she'd get off Wish! *Wishing* she look good when she really look like a big ass *Amazon*!" Anita yelled out causing the crowd to bust out laughing over the music.

Taking advantage of the attention, I slowly turned around and stepped over to her, close enough to stare down at her with intimidation. Surprisingly, this bold bitch didn't flinch nor buck. In fact, Anita put her hands on her hips and dared me to jump bad.

"Little girl, you don't want this! Trust me when I say you better quit while you're ahead!" I warned as Katrice clinched onto my arm to try and hold me back.

"You right bitch! Don't *NOBODY* want none of that!" Anita hollered with her mouth wide open before I closed it with my fist.

As she laid lifeless on the cold nasty floor of the hole in the wall club, everything got quiet until folks started assuming she was dead. Shaking my head, I knew better!

Taking the glass of ice water off the table next to me, I dashed it down onto Anita's face causing her to snap out of the daze I put her in. The embarrassment that shone all over her was enough for me.

"Look at the bitch scrambling for the door!" Katrice laughed along with the whole crowd. "It's about time you stood up for yourself again Cashay!"

"I told you earlier sis! I ain't taking no more shit from those bitches!" I reminded her. "I meant that shit! New year, new me boo!"

As Katrice and I stood there getting a good laugh out of the situation, I felt a presence behind me. Before I could spin around to see who it was, my best friend made a surprised expression that made my stomach flutter.

"Who is this?" Katrice sang as I turned to face this tall handsome stranger that reminded me of Trevor Jackson.

"I have no idea?" I giggled and stared over his six-foot frame from head to toe. His smooth milk chocolate skin was flawless, and his facial hairs were groomed to a 'T'. Oh, how I loved a bearded man. It was trimmed perfectly too. Not too long. Not too bushy.

"I'm Damarr and I don't mean to overstep my boundaries or disrespect you in any way ma, but don't eva think that you have to defend yourself when someone teases you about your size… because in my eyes, everything about you is beautiful," he spoke while stroking the waves on his tapered cut.

When I say that my ass was in a straight daze, I wasn't lying because this nigga's mesmerizing voice spewing out those compliments had me feeling myself. Blushing and all, I thanked him and introduced myself and Katrice.

"Always hold you head up high cuz you're a beautiful black queen," Damarr grinned and reached for my hand.

Kissing it gently with those soft, full lips had me ready to jump his damn bones. Normally I would fear that I would hurt a nigga if I did some shit like that, but this man standing in front of me... I knew he could handle all of this! He may have had me by a couple of inches, but I definitely had him by more than a couple of pounds.

"Thank you and I sure will!" I giggled as Katrice nudged me in the side with her elbow.

"Girl he's fine!" she whispered just as Damarr released my hand.

"Yes, yes he is!" I spoke boldly getting us an invite to his table.

"You sho' got that southern drawl, but you not from around here huh?" Katrice questioned after we all sat down. "I sho' ain't seen you before."

"I was born and raised here, but when my mama died, I moved to Arkansas to stay with my grandmother on my daddy's side. This is my first time back in 15 years."

Now, I didn't know what brought him back to Houston, but I was curious as hell. This man actually had me intrigued beyond belief.

"What you come back out here for now?" Katrice asked nosily making me kick her under the table.

Sure, I was wondering the same thing, but I wasn't about to ask him. I was going to wait for him to volunteer the information on his own.

"What?!" she hissed. "I just wanted to know! Don't you?"

"It's cool!" Damarr laughed and ordered us a round of drinks then waited for the waitress to step away before he continued. "Unfortunately, I came here because of a death in my family..."

"Oh! I'm so sorry!" Katrice apologized and covered her mouth.

"Nah, you're good. No need to apologize cuz you didn't know. It's cool," he replied and downed his drink as soon as they arrived at the table. "I came out here when they found my sister dead a couple of weeks ago..."

"Who was your sister?" Katrice asked.

I wanted to kick her ass again for inquiring about that. "Terra Moss..."

"Oh wow! Terra Moss was your sister?" I asked. I didn't know the girl personally, but I did recall seeing something about it on the news.

"Yea, she was my older sister. I ain't seen her in years. Once crack got her ass at 16, it was a wrap. Rehab, church, going cold turkey... nothing could help her," he said shaking his head. "We laid her to rest last weekend."

My mood shifted from freaky to sad and now I was sitting there feeling bad about Katrice even questioning him about it. I wanted to apologize, but when I opened my mouth to say the words, Damarr asked me if I had a man.

Talk about changing the subject and the mood! I guess he didn't want to think about what he was going through and maybe I could help take his mind off things. Just maybe...

"No, she don't have no man!" Katrice blurted out. She was slurring a bit, so I knew that she was lit.

"No, I'm not in a relationship at the moment and right now, it looks like I need to get my friend back to the house!" I laughed trying to downplay the fact that I might have to help Katrice to the car.

Since she rarely drank, when she did, she couldn't handle it. If I wasn't so much in Damarr's face, I would've noticed that she had four empty shot glasses in front of her.

"I'm not ready to go yet!" She giggled and whipped out her cell to take pictures. "I wanna play matchmaker and hook you two up! You guys will make the perfect couple! Y'all look so cute together!"

"Cut it out!" I laughed.

"Nah, it's cool!" Damarr insisted as he scooted closer to me and wrapped his arm around my shoulder.

The sensual scent of his cologne had me squirming in my damn seat. That along with the warmness of his skin on mine was driving me crazy!

It had been months since I last got some and being close to this fine ass brutha wasn't making it any better. All I could do was pray that I didn't go jumping the gun and sleep with him on the first night!

Please! Please Lord help me!

Chapter Two

Damarr Taylor

When I got back to Houston to bury my sister, I wasn't looking to get into anything. Especially after getting out of a bad relationship just a few months prior.

When it came to dating, I was terrible at the shit. Always going for these model type chicks for appearance purposes. It was always the same with them. The more attractive they were, the more they wanted. The newest designer handbag, expensive jewelry, hair, and nails done, but didn't want to lift a finger to cook, clean, or even surprise a nigga with a gift every now and then.

Sadly, all the females that I had dated were always on some bullshit and I was done with that. I was ready to go after what really turned me on and that was a chick with some meat on her bones. For a big guy like myself, I needed someone thick to hold on to. Not a damn bone with implants on top and bottom. I didn't care what the next nigga said... that shit didn't feel the same and it wasn't natural.

Now this Cashay chick I met, everything about her was natural and it was very attractive.

She rocked her own shoulder length curly hair, and she had God given curves that made a nigga's head spin.

Taking that chance stepping to her was the best move I had made in a long time and something about it just felt right. So right that I invited her back to my suite.

"I'm totally fine to drive and... as good and tempting as that sounds, I gotta get my homegirl back home. Maybe we can hook up tomorrow or something?"

Disappointment swept over me, but I kept a straight face. "Cool, take my number and give me a call when you can."

Leaving the club that night, I couldn't stop thinking about that chick. I almost got mad at myself for not getting her number because I wanted to reach out and at least shoot her a text or something.

Cashay must've been thinking the same thing because soon as I showered and laid in the bed, my cell was chirping with a message from her. She was thanking me for the kind words and letting me know that she was praying for me! She even told me to let her know if there was anything that she could do for me!

Made my fucking eyes water and I hadn't shed a tear in a long time. Not even when they found my sister Terra dead.

"This girl praying for me?!" I whispered shaking my head in disbelief. "She don't even know me and she's concerned about what I'm going through! Ain't this some shit!"

A chick with a pure heart was hard to find and I didn't know how true that was with Cashay, but she was getting off to a great fucking start. With a smile on my face, I sent her a text back to thank her as well as let her know that I appreciated her.

The unexplainable feeling that came over me as we exchanged messages for the next hour had me anxious to see her again. I just wanted to be around her and enjoy her company.

Ring, buzz, ring...

Just as I was about to respond to Cashay's message saying goodnight, Chandra was calling me. Seeing her name pop up on my screen made me mad all over again.

"What the fuck are you calling me for?" I snapped ready to hang back up and block her.

"Why you gotta be so mean to me Damarr?" she whined. "You know I love you!"

"I'm mean because I caught you stealing my fucking money!"

"You weren't gonna miss that lil' ten grand Damarr and I didn't steal it! You left all that money in the box and you said it was for emergencies!" Chandra yelled. "I had an emergency!"

"An emergency is getting me out of fucking jail if I got popped or some shit! Not to treat your homegirls to a shopping spree! I was fucking you, not yo' whole fucking crew!" I shot back. "Look, it was good while it lasted. I let you keep that 'lil' ten grand' and you got all yo' shit outta my spot, so we ain't got shit else to say to each other Chandra. I'm good."

"Don't make me come over there and bust all the windows out of every last one of yo' cars nigga! You know I ain't playing with you!"

"Go on over there and you ain't gonna find shit but a 'for sale' sign in the front yard! I'm done with you and Arkansas!"

Hanging up on her, I blocked her number and deleted all her contact information from my phone. Didn't nobody have time for a thieving ass gold digger. At least I didn't!

"I know this bitch ain't called me from another number!" I gritted as my cell rang soon as I set it down, but when I saw the new contact that I had already stored into my phone, I knew who it was.

"Hey!" Cashay sang out. "You didn't respond when I said goodnight, so I just called to make sure you were good."

Grinning widely, I rubbed my beard and laid back on my pillow. The sound of this chick's concern filled voice had me wanting to hold a whole conversation and learn more about her.

"Look at you! Checkin' on a nigga already. I like that shit."

"Well, you seem so nice, and I hate to see someone as sweet and kind as you are going through something so terrible," Cashay spoke sincerely.

"I don't know about all that sweet and kind shit, but I am a pretty chill dude," I admitted with a laugh. "You know everyone has two sides."

"So, you saying you have a bad side?!" she shrieked.

"I'm saying I have the side you saw tonight, but I also have a hard side because I work in the streets."

"So, that's it? That's all to you? No in between?"

"Yea, but that's the side that only my family or the woman I'm in love with gets to see."

That shit shut Cashay up and she was speechless for the next few seconds. Quickly breaking the silence, I spoke up.

"Why you got quiet?"

"Uh, I don't know. I guess I wasn't expecting that answer. That's all."

"Is that a good or bad thing?" I pressed.

"Definitely good. All good for sure!" She giggled.

That night we talked for hours on the phone and really got to know each other. When we hung up, I was so tired that I passed out and overslept the next morning.

"Fuck!" I said when I saw all the missed calls from my folks. One from my uncle, two from my great aunt and seven from my cousin.

Instead of returning any of their calls, I showered, and shot over to my grandmothers. My late mother's auntie was on the front porch of her sister's house like she was waiting for me to get there so she could cuss me out.

"Damarr! I told you we were doing an early lunch today. You were supposed to be here at nine to help! Got us all in here waiting on you! You know Ma'Dear ain't gonna let nobody eat until her favorite baby gets here! You get on my damn nerves!"

Auntie Dell went on and on about her sister but was laughing the whole time. Soon as I got on the porch, she hugged me tightly then slapped me on the ass and shooed me inside.

"Hey y'all! Damarr finally made it!" she yelled out just as my cell buzzed.

Drawing it out my pocket, I checked the 'good morning' text that Cashay had sent.

"Who got you grinning like that nigga?!" my younger cousin clowned popping me in the head.

"Stop Demisha!" I gritted ready to pop her back. She played way too fucking much and I wasn't with it. We were grown!

"None of yo' business! Where's your baby daddy? Any of them? Don't you got like three?! That's who you need to be worried about!" I clowned causing my Uncle Terry to crack up.

"You know they all locked up or dead. That child right there is just like her mama! A fucking Black Widow! She kills anything she touches!" Uncle Terry teased as he rolled by in his wheelchair.

Laughing as I glanced at my cell, I saw that Cashay was calling. Demisha's nosy ass was all in my face.

"Damn cousin! Back up!"

"Who is that? Got you all grinning and shit! You ain't been in town but five days and you done knocked one already Damarr?!" Demisha clowned.

"It's this chick I met, why?"

"What's her name?"

"Why are you being so nosy?" I inquired.

"Cuz I'm just wondering if I know her, that's all!"

"Her name is Cashay."

Demisha spit the Coca Cola out her mouth as if she was surprised.

"You know her?" I asked.

Instead of responding with a yes or no, Demisha started talking shit. She was calling Cashay all kinds of fat bitches and the whole time I was staring at her big ass. I mean, she had no reason to call anybody fat. It was like the pot calling the kettle black.

"You done put on quite a bit of weight yourself, so you have no place to be talking shit Demisha," I laughed. "As a matter of fact, I think you might be bigger than her!"

"You's a lie nigga!"

"When was the last time you saw her?"

"It's been years, but I know I ain't bigger than that cow!" Demisha retorted.

"Wow! Why you gotta call shorty all outta her name and shit though?"

"Because that's what the bitch is, and I hope you ain't planning on fucking her because she'll probably squash yo ass!" she said as she rolled her eyes. "You tall as fuck and still only got that big ho by a couple of inches at the most! And as big as her titties, ass, hips, thighs and gut are, she'll definitely smash you in more than one way cuddy!"

"Ain't none of what I plan on doing with that woman any of your business! I like the chick, so your opinion don't matter to me one bit! I ain't never told you who to lay with when you was making babies huh?"

"Damn! You so defensive cuz!" Demisha said. "Out of all the bitches you could've chosen to fuck with, I can't believe you chose Cashay!"

"Don't you worry about it," I said. "You the one who came all up on me, eyeing my fucking cell down trying to see who was calling me!"

"Okay, y'all calm down in my house!" Ma'Dear demanded as she strode in. "Demisha, I know you not talking shit to my baby!"

My grandmother walked over and wrapped her arms around me. After giving her a warm hug, I kissed her cheek. "Wow! You really gon' do me like that granny?" Demisha asked.

"You always starting something with somebody!" Ma'Dear argued. "Where yo kids at? You need to keep an eye on them with their lil bad asses!"

"My kids are playing in the backyard granny and they're not bad. They're just a little misunderstood," Demisha clarified.

"A little misunderstood my ass!" Uncle Terry responded. "Them some bad ass muthafuckas!"

"Whatever Uncle Terry! No disrespect but nobody asked for your two cents," Demisha responded.

"Well, I figured since you was over here giving your unwanted advice to Damarr, I could offer mine to you," Uncle Terry clowned. "If you don't want nobody giving you advice then don't offer none."

I loved my Uncle Terry, especially at times like these. He was always quick to put somebody in their place no matter who they were. I appreciated that about him because he never let anybody step on his toes... not that some shit like that would be easy to do considering he was in a wheelchair.

"Enough of that arguing!" Ma'Dear shouted out. "We came here to enjoy some good food, so let's do that. Damarr baby, I'm glad you're here."

"Me too Ma'Dear! Sorry I'm late," I apologized as I embraced her again.

"As long as you're here."

We all gathered around the counter where there were pans of food spread out. There was fried chicken, stuffed pork, spiral honey ham, homemade cornbread, collard greens, potato salad, homemade mac and cheese, black eyed peas, dirty rice, and homemade dinner rolls. For dessert there was a huge pan of peach cobbler and another one with bread pudding. Let me tell you, when these black folks got together, they definitely threw down in the kitchen.

After we piled our plates high, we headed to the dining room then all sat down to eat and chat for the next couple of hours. I enjoyed spending time with my family, but I couldn't get my mind off of Cashay. As soon as I left my Ma'Dear's house, I hit her up. I just wanted to see her, smell her, touch her if she'd let me. I knew I just met her last night, but there was something about her that had me wanting to be all up inside her.

"Hello," she answered practically purring through the phone.

"Hey Cashay. I was just thinking about you, so I thought I'd hit you up and see what you were up to," I said.

"Aw, that's sweet of you. I'm not doing much. What are you up to?"

"Just leaving my grandmother's place for Sunday dinner, well lunch," I said as I chuckled.

"I thought your grandmother lived in Arkansas?"

"That's my dad's mother. This one is on my mother's side."

"Oh, okay," she laughed. "How was your early Sunday Dinner? You know we cook early on Sunday's around here!"

"Right! I'm stuffed like a Thanksgiving turkey." I laughed and so did she. "I got you a plate."

"You lying!" she scoffed.

"No, seriously. I told you I was thinking about you."

"Wow! I appreciate that," she said, and I could hear the sincerity in her tone.

"So, can I bring it over or would you like to come pick it up?"

"Well, if it's all the same to you, I'll come by and get it," she offered.

"Don't want me to know where you live yet huh?" I asked jokingly even though I was serious.

"Well, we did just meet last night…"

"Right, but I have no problem giving you my address."

Even though I had just moved back to the area, I had rented a home with the option to buy in the Katy area. The reason I rented the house as opposed to buying it was because I needed to make sure I liked the area and got along with my neighbors. I watched the ID channel on a regular basis, and *Fear Thy Neighbor* was one of my favorite shows. However, as much as I enjoyed the show, I was not looking to be featured on it as one of the dead nor was I trying to be locked up behind no bullshit.

Although I had only been staying here for a week, I had no complaints. So far, so good.

"Well, if you send it to me, I can come over in a couple of hours," she responded.

"Okay, bet! See you soon."

We ended the call, and I had the nerve to get excited about seeing her. That wasn't like me. Usually, I paid a chick to give me some space. It wasn't like that with Cashay though. She had me feeling different.

Since I wasn't really close to any of my family that was close to my age, I didn't have nobody to talk about Cashay to except Demisha. Although she was my cousin, speaking to her about this chick wasn't the answer.

The way she talked shit about Cashay? Nah, that wasn't a smart thing to do.

Choosing to move on my own terms, I decided that I was just going to spend the time needed getting to know Cashay. After all, there was nothing that Demisha could say that would deter my thinking.

Certain that I wanted to get to know this woman, I wasn't going to let the fact that my cousin didn't like her stand in my way.

Or anyone else for that matter...

Chapter Three

Katrice

While Cashay chatted on the phone with the guy we met at the club, I made myself comfortable on the sofa waiting to watch some television with her. The only reason why I paused the movie was because she acted like she really wanted to watch it so bad.

"Hey boo!" Cashay spoke cheerfully as she reentered the room grinning widely. "I guess I won't be watching that movie with you after all."

"What? Why not?" I asked.

"I have a date," she said still cheesing showing off her pearly whites.

"What do you mean you have a date?"

"That's what I said."

"So, you're going out with the guy you met last night?" I inquired as I anxiously followed her to her bedroom to get all the tea. I was not expecting things to move that quickly between them.

"Yes!"

"Well, where are you two going?" I questioned as I sat on the bed.

"I'm going to his place. He went to Sunday dinner at his grandmother's house, and he made me a plate, so I'm going there to get it," she informed sending a red flag up. I mean, sure I wanted her to date this handsome man, but for her to be going over to his house alone like that? I wasn't feeling that shit.

"So, you're going to a strange man's house?" I asked. "Why y'all ain't meeting somewhere public?"

"Wait." Cashay laughed. "I thought you wanted me to hook up with this dude! You were all for it last night at the club! Why are you acting like this now?"

"I am all for it... or I was until you said you were going to his house and you don't even know him girl! He's a stranger until then!"

"Okay, first of all, I'm grown! I've been on plenty of dates before to know how to handle myself and if you're that concerned Katrice, I'll text you his address and his damn license plate number when I get there! If it makes you feel any better!" Cashay huffed. "You know I can handle myself and this stun gun too! If he tries anything funny, I'll zap him then stomp him while he's down and continue to do so while I wait on the cops and medics to save him!"

"Wow Cashay! Is it really worth risking all that to go over there just to get a damn plate of food?!"

"I'm not risking shit Katrice! If anything, I might be passing up a great opportunity to get to know a wonderful guy! Besides, he was thoughtful enough to make me a plate of food! The least I can do is go get it."

"Why couldn't he have just dropped it off to you?"

"Well, I don't have my own place..."

"So, just because he does, it's a great place to meet up so soon?"

"Look Katrice, since we share this house, I just thought it would be less awkward and uncomfortable if I went to his place. It's not that big of a deal," she said.

"Right! Until we see your face plastered on the news as a missing person!" I exclaimed.

The guy was handsome and all, but she didn't know that nigga from the cow that jumped over the moon. I didn't think she was making a wise decision by going over to his house. Anything could happen to her over there. She wasn't thinking straight.

Expecting Cashay to take me seriously was wrong on my part because she stood there and busted out laughing like I had just told the funniest joke ever. Poor child didn't have a clue or didn't want to take one.

"Uh, that wasn't meant to be funny," I replied and cut my eyes.

"Maybe not, but it was. That man is not a threat to me," she assured me when she didn't know herself. "He's really nice and caring."

"And you know that from meeting him that one time."

"Well, we had a phone conversation that lasted well into the night. I feel I know a little about him and what I know I like. I wanna get to know him better, which is why I agreed to go there..."

"No, you agreed to go because he bribed you with a plate of food!" I barked. The look on her face made me immediately regret what I said.

"Wow!" she said with a hurtful expression that made me feel even worse. "Well, I guess the way to a big girl's heart is through her stomach, right?"

"I didn't mean..."

"It's okay Katrice. No need to explain because I understand exactly what you meant. If you don't mind, I'd like to finish getting ready," she spoke softly.

"Cashay, you know I didn't mean to hurt your feelings," I replied in an effort to smooth things over.

"It's cool sis. I ain't trippin'!" Her mouth may have said the words, but her facial expression definitely said something totally different.

Rather than continue to try and explain myself when she already had her mind made up, I decided to leave the room and give her some time to cool off. Maybe once she figured out that I meant no harm, she'd speak to me again without thinking I insulted her.

Going back to the living room, I sat on the sofa. Minutes later, Cashay exited the bedroom and walked right by me while I was still watching

TV. She went straight out the front door and didn't even tell me goodbye, see me later or nothing!

The way she left like that made me feel some kind of way because we barely ever argued. However, when we did it was always pertaining to her weight because Cashay had so many insecurities.

Maybe I wasn't making it any better by the rude remarks, but she knew how I was. I would never do or say anything purposely to hurt her feelings. She knew that, so I didn't understand why she took what I said so seriously.

It seemed as though the only time me and Cashay had issues was when there was a man involved. She acted like she had to be wanted by a man so badly that she made bad decisions.

If she had more confidence and self-esteem, she wouldn't be so damn easy! That man wanted her last night because he saw how beautiful she was, and last night she reeked of confidence. I just wanted her to be like that every day, but I knew it was going to be hard for her. She had been bullied so much when we were younger that those insecurities often came back to life.

Sending Cashay a text telling her to enjoy herself was to ensure that she didn't think that I was hating on her. Truthfully, maybe I was. Hell, while I was talking shit about her not having a man in months, I hadn't either! The last guy that I went out with was Dudley and that was a long time ago.

With a name like that, I should've known to stay away. If I had, I wouldn't have slept with a married man. Especially one who had six kids and a crazy wife!

Damn, I really did like that dude and missed the hell out of having sex with him too. Not only did he have a nice long, thick dick, he knew how to put it down just like I liked it!

"I need to get me some business so that I can stay out of Cashay's!" I told myself trying my best not to feel jealous.

Becoming borderline desperate, I got on my laptop and joined a black single's group on a social network. The first step that was required once accepted into the group was to post a pic and give three fun facts about yourself. Okay, that was easy.

Scrolling through my many selfies, I chose my favorite photo and posted it. The caption with my fun facts read: **Outgoing, Independent, Open to new things.**

That post right there got me all the unwanted attention that I wasn't looking for. It took me two hours to sort through the weirdos before I found a few that might be worth replying back to.

"Jacob? Hmmmm, you are fine as hell and your profile looks good too!" I whispered to myself as I opened a new window to do a little search using his name and photo.

Within minutes, I found out that he had two baby mamas and a shit load of drama that came with it. His Facebook profile told it all!

"Delete!" I laughed and went on to the next guy on my list. "Baylor?"

Repeating the same steps on this fine sexy hunk of a guy, I quickly discovered that he was gay as hell! All the pics on his personal page was with rainbows or with other guys. Oh, and the way he was posing with some of them!

No thank you! I'll pass.

The last on my list was a very handsome musician who went by 'Legend' Terry. These men and their names! What were their mothers thinking when they came up with this wild shit?

Well, whatever his name was, his picture did him justice. All of them! Even the ones he took in the bed when he first woke up!

His shoulder length dreads were always on point and so was his body! So, why was he all up in my inbox? What made him choose me? Not saying that I was ugly or anything, but with as many followers as he had and as many bitches that were sweating him on his Facebook and Instagram pages... why me?

Curious as hell, I reread his question asking me to tell more about myself. Without thinking twice, I lied to him about my physical appearance to see if he would still be interested. Now, if this dude still wanted to get with me after thinking that I had ugly feet and ugly scars on my legs from my childhood and was still scared of the dark at my age, he was a keeper.

"What?!" I screamed. "Did this man say that he would take care of my feet for me?!"

Legend must've really wanted some to be feeding me some bullshit like that. But I couldn't lie, that same bullshit had me intrigued and wanting to know more about him. So, instead of continuing to play this game with him, I agreed to see him that evening at the Soul Fest that was taking place on the fairgrounds.

Now that right there, I could definitely do!

Chapter Four

Legend

When I saw Katrice's name pop up as a new member in the single's group on Facebook, I was reminded of the crush I used to have on her when we were kids. Shit, I thought she was cute back then, but when she posted a new pic of her today, I was like damn! This chic was beautiful.

"I wonder if she's gonna remember me?" I laughed to myself.

It had been years since we had seen each other, and I had definitely changed on the outside and she only knew me by Lucca James. Once Katrice heard that name, she would surely remember me from music class when she stood up for me. She was always standing up for someone when they were getting picked on.

Although I thought it was nice and everything, I had to show everyone that a girl didn't have to stand up for me. They all knew it to be true when I had to beat the shit out of Timothy Branch after school that day.

"Damn!" I smiled as I got myself ready for my second set of the day.

Being the leader of this local band got me mad attention, and I loved what I did. Singing and the guitar were my life. The only thing that was missing was someone to share it with.

Most men at my age, in my position wouldn't be thinking about settling down, but growing up in a two- parent household made me know better. The single life wasn't what it was cracked up to be.

Between the groupies and the gold diggers, I had yet to find a chick to dig me for me. I wanted someone who wanted me from what was on the inside, not on the outside.

Reminding myself of my worth, I took the stage and did what I did. When I finished, I went straight to the makeshift dressing room. It wasn't much, but it was private.

Shooting Katrice a text, I let her know just where to meet me on the fairgrounds. I wanted to see her before my last set so that I could make sure she was up front when I sang my new song.

Right on time, she showed up on the entertainment lawn area looking more fucking beautiful than the pictures she posted online. As our eyes met, she stared at me strangely.

"Legend?"

"Yea, that's me." I smiled and hesitated.

"Damn, you look familiar!"

"You remember Lucca James?" I asked still grinning as Katrice stood there thinking. "From music class?"

"Loo-Kuh!"?!" she laughed pronouncing my name properly then hugged me tightly. "No! No fucking way! I can't believe it!"

"Yea, I couldn't believe it when I saw your pic on Facebook!" I admitted.

"So, that's why you inboxed me?! You could've just told me who you were!" She giggled. "But I do appreciate this pass though! I get to enjoy the… wait a damn minute! Legend… you play with the group, 'Choice', huh?"

"Yes, I'm the lead…"

"Why didn't I put two and two together?" Katrice teased and stood there acting starstruck. It was just me, so she didn't have to behave like I was a celebrity and then have me feeling uncomfortable.

"Stop tripping Katrice. You act like you ain't known me for years."

"But I ain't seen you in years either! I don't know whether to call you Lucca or Legend!"

"Whatever you feel comfortable calling me as long as I can call you beautiful," I flirted and licked my lips.

Why did I go and do that shit?! Katrice looked like she was about to pass out.

Quickly pulling it together, she started stuttering to reply. "Boy, stop playing!"

"Let me tell you what. Why don't I go out here on this stage and prove to you how much of a man I am and show you that I definitely ain't playing," I teased again and walked away just as I heard my name being called.

Handling my business, I got up there and did what I did best. It worked like a charm too. Had Katrice standing up teary eyed and everything.

Rushing me when I finished and stepped down from the stage, she greeted me with a hug then thanked me for inviting her. "That last song was so beautiful."

"Just like you. That was why I had to sing it for you," I confessed and bent down to embrace her.

"That was for me? Damn! And I thought I was tripping because when you sang it, it felt like it was just for me and what I've been going through."

"Just know that brighter days are coming. You just gotta believe baby," I encouraged with a smile. "Now what are you doing after this?"

"I was going home, but after the high you just gave me, I don't want it to end!" she told me.

"And it don't have to, baby."

Clinching Katrice's hand tightly, I led her through the gates with security ahead of us. She found out just why when the crowd went wild. As usual there were a few bold chicks that went above and beyond to be seen and heard, even if that meant showing their titties. Shit was crazy!

"What the hell?!" Katrice shouted as we went to my truck. "I don't see how you go through that shit every time you perform! I couldn't do it!

"That's why I don't have a girl now. This life ain't for everybody."

Although the band I was a part of was local, we were well known on the internet around the world. We had gone on tour several times, but that shit was exhausting. It felt damn good to be home. Houston was where my heart was.

"I totally understand." She laughed and then asked about her car that was parked in the lot two blocks down. "I need to get it before they tow it. They have a three-hour limit."

Driving her over there, she had me follow her to her crib so that she could leave her car there. It wasn't that far, and the ride gave me time to think of what to do with Katrice.

"Okay, she gotta nice place," I whispered to myself as we arrived at her house.

After she got out and held up her finger, she ran inside and came out a few minutes later with a jacket. It was getting breezy, but shit, I would've kept her warm.

"You good?" I asked as Katrice hopped in my truck smiling and smelling good. I could tell she freshened up and I got anxious to get up on her.

Taking my time, I held back and asked if she wanted to get something to eat. When she agreed, I chose the restaurant only because it was useless to ask a female where she wanted to eat. They never could make their minds up.

Brenner's on the Bayou was lowkey and located on Houston's Buffalo Bayou. Calling ahead, I reserved the 'Red Room' for privacy. That way, I could avoid any interruptions when Katrice and I ate and caught up.

"This place is nice! I've never been here before! Wait until I tell Cashay about this!" she gasped as we were shown to our private dining room.

Katrice took pictures until I stood beside her to be in one. Now she was acting embarrassed, but it calmed her down enough to sit and order some food.

While we waited for it to come, I asked her about Cashay. "Y'all still tight huh?"

Katrice got serious and told me about how when her mother died, Cashay's mom took her in. They were like sisters.

"I remember that! It's good to see y'all still tight. Most people grow up and grow apart. Shit, I don't kick it with none of the folks that I used to hang out with back in the day. They are either married, locked up or dead. Real shit."

"Real sad shit!" Katrice sighed as the waitress brought our food and drinks.

As we ate and chatted, I realized that I was actually comfortable with her. She was really chill, and I could see myself dating her.

"How was your food?"

"It was good, but I'm full," she said as she smiled and thanked me.

"You wanna walk down to the Blue Bar and have one last drink before they close?" I asked.

"What's the Blue Bar?"

"Come on," I urged and walked around the table to help her up.

Strolling down to the restaurant's bar on the bayou hand in hand, Katrice and I enjoyed the beautiful view. It was nice, but of course, a damn groupie had to come fuck it up with her rude ass attitude. The chick came all between us and knocked our hands apart.

"Legend! Legend!" she hollered and damn near tackled me.

It surprised the shit out of me when Katrice heaved the petite female off me and checked her verbally. "You might've gotten a damn picture or autograph if you wouldn't have run over here acting like a damn fool! What the hell is wrong with folks?"

By then, security had picked the girl up and taken her out. Shaking my head at her, I turned to see Katrice frowned up.

"I'm ready to go. That bitch done spoiled my whole night!"

"I'm sorry about that shit," I apologized, but what could I do?

The only way to ensure that it didn't happen again was to have security with me 24/7 again and I didn't want that. It not only brought too much attention, but I didn't have a bit of fucking privacy!

Leaving Brenner's at closing, I went ahead and drove Katrice home. She was quiet during the ride which made me question if she was having second thoughts about fucking with me.

To see where her head was, I asked her if I could take her to breakfast the next morning. Katrice turned to me so fast and shook her head no.

"You can either come to my house and I'll cook, or I can come to your place. Being seen with you in public is way too much for me. I be done caught a fucking case for beating down one of your fans!" she clowned as I parked in front of her place.

"You are funny, you know that?" I flirted and eyed her down lustfully.

"Am I?" she challenged.

"You are, but you're beautiful too. Did I already tell you that shit?"

"Yea, but I'll never get tired of hearing you say it Lucca," she replied with a smile as she got out and blew me a kiss.

"Damn, you not gonna let me walk you to the door? It's dark out here," I asked.

"Thanks, but I got it," she said running to open it up.

Waving at me, she yelled out 'goodbye' then disappeared inside. Seeing the lights cut on, I went on and headed home.

Just as I hit the block, my cell chimed. It was a message from Katrice.

Katrice: Thanks again Lucca! I really enjoyed myself! Be safe and I'll see you around nine in the morning!

After checking out the 'kiss' emoji, I couldn't stop myself from grinning as I confirmed our breakfast date. It was something about Katrice that drew me in just like when we were kids. That shit had me intrigued like a muthafucka!

Yea, I gotta to explore this shit with Katrice a little more. I definitely do!

Chapter Five

Cashay

Katrice came running in my room late at night waking me up. She was yelling and screaming so loudly that I couldn't even tell her about my date with Damarr first. She was too busy trying to tell me where she had been.

Truthfully, I was still salty with Katrice about the disrespectful shit that she said before I left out. Sure, she apologized, but it still was bothering me. If she was so close to me and called herself my sister, why would she even talk to me like that? I couldn't figure that shit out for nothing!

"Cashay! Guess who I just went on a date with?" she hollered still bouncing up and down.

"Who?! Just tell me before you give yourself a damn heart attack! You done woke me up outta my sleep, so just tell me already Katrice!" I huffed and sat up in the bed. "I'm tired as hell, so I don't have time for guessing games in the middle of the night!"

I didn't mean to snap on her, but like I said, I was still salty with her behavior earlier. I mean, when I left, she didn't have a date. Hell, she wasn't even dating anyone. So, I was curious to know who she went out on a date with tonight. More importantly, I wondered was she as careful with her date as she was trying to advise me.

"Lucca! Lucca James!"

As I laid there, I had to think back for a little bit. The name sounded familiar, but I couldn't recall where I remembered him from.

After a couple of minutes, it finally dawned on me. "You mean that little scrawny nerdy looking dude that went to school with us who was always singing and shit? The one who wore those thick black Coke bottle glasses with the tape in the middle?" I cracked up then remembered the fight. "Oh, the one who beat the shit outta Timothy Branch?!"

"Yes! That's the one!" She smiled and danced around.

"So, why the hell would you get so excited about going out with that nerd?" I asked as Katrice whipped out her cell and showed me a pic of her and this fine ass nigga with dreads. "Is that him?! That looks like that one dude that sings in that group! What's his name?"

"Legend?!" she questioned and waited for me to figure out that Lucca was Legend. That shit was crazy!

"You are fucking kidding me?!" I started yelling with her.

"No, I went to the fair and saw him perform! He gave me a pass and even sang a song for me! Oh, then he took me out to this fancy restaurant!" she screamed then began to look sad.

"What's wrong? What happened?"

"It's just all that attention from all those females! I don't think I could date him on the regular!" Katrice confessed then turned around and told me that he was coming over for breakfast in the morning.

Talking about getting excited! I had to get on the phone and call Damarr to tell him all about it. Only when I did, he didn't answer.

"Oh, my bad Cashay," Katrice said. "I forgot to ask you how it went today when you went over Damarr's?"

"Well, it actually went quite well boo!" I confessed without going into details.

"I'm so glad you did!"

"Thanks Katrice!"

"I guess I'm not gonna get any details, huh?"

"It wasn't any spectacular compared to yours, but we got to know a lot about each other and that was nice. Oh, and the food from his grandmother's house was the bomb!" I said as I smiled.

Anytime a man could offer good company and great food, I was there. Damarr was such a gentleman last night. He didn't try anything funny, and he wasn't a pervert. After I ate, we chilled and watched Netflix for a couple of hours before he walked me out to my car.

Once we were outside, he asked me if he could kiss me. Of course, I said yes. I just wanted to feel his luscious lips on mine. I wanted to see if they were as soft and juicy as they looked.

When he touched my chin and tilted my face upward, I was not disappointed. He pressed his lips to mine and gently brushed my lips. I wanted to wrap my arms around his neck and pull him closer, but I didn't want to seem desperate. The kiss was short and sweet and before I knew it, it was over.

I wasn't upset though. This man had my whole insides tingling. He made me feel amazing all the way to my toes.

"I'ma hit you up tomorrow," he said in a sexy and husky voice.

"Okay," I said in a voice barely above a whisper.

However, when Katrice questioned me about whether we kissed or not, I lied. After the exchange we had before I left, I wasn't ready to share that with her just yet.

"Of course, we didn't kiss! I don't know him like that! I may have been excited about seeing him last night but I ain't that desperate to be locking lips with him so soon," I lied.

"Well, I can't even lie girl, I definitely wanted to kiss Lucca last night! Just being that close to him had me feeling all these strange feelings... whew chile!" she said as she fanned her face.

All I could do was laugh. I mean, who was I to judge her? If I hadn't controlled myself the way that I did last night, I probably wouldn't have come home at all. Just kidding! Damarr was way too much of a gentleman for that.

"So, did y'all make another date?" she asked.

"We're gonna talk some time tomorrow."

"Well, I'll let you get some rest. I'm sorry that I woke you, but I was just so excited."

"It's cool. We'll talk tomorrow," I said.

"It is tomorrow, but later girl!" she said as she bounced her happy tail out the door.

Laying back down, I scooted under the covers and closed my eyes. Sleep didn't take long to envelope me again.

****

The next morning, the shrill ringing of my alarm jarred me from my sleep. I jumped up and slid out of bed. I had to get myself together for work. Dealing with my kiddos was what I loved. I didn't have kids of my own, but I loved kids so what better job could I have than to be a schoolteacher. It was the perfect job for me!

Teaching seventh grade at Cinco Ranch Junior High School, was my position. It was about an hour away from our house, but I didn't mind the drive.

"Let me hurry up!" I whispered to myself as I finished getting dressed.

After I fixed my cup of coffee, I headed out the door without saying goodbye to Katrice. Only because she worked as a law clerk and had to be at work an hour later than I did, so we often didn't see one another until the evening.

"What now?" I huffed. "I can't check now, so whoever it is, they're gonna have to wait!"

I was halfway to the school when my phone alerted me that I had a text message. As much as I wanted to see who it was, I decided against it. There was no way I was going to text while driving.

With curiosity of message, I checked it soon as I made it to the middle school campus. "Yes!" I cheered as I checked the screen. I was excited to see that it was a message from Damarr. I smiled as I opened it...

Damarr: Good morning. I was just thinking about you. I thought I'd drop you a line and wish you a great day!!

"Aww! He's so sweet," I gushed to myself.

"Cashay, who you talking to?" Lena Burnes asked.

"Girl myself!" I said as we busted out laughing.

"It is way too early for that mess!" she responded back.

"You're right!"

We walked together to the inside of the school. Once inside, I went to check my box for any announcements or paperwork put in by the copy room clerk. After I got the things from my box and headed to my room, I was thankful that I didn't have duty until this afternoon.

Taking a moment to respond to Damarr's text, I quickly checked the clock on the far wall. By the time it was displaying, I had 15 minutes before the bell rang for the students to come in.

Me: Hey yourself! Thank you for the morning message. It really put a smile on my face. I'm at work right now, and my kids are about to come in class so I'll text you when I get home. Enjoy your day *smiley face*

He responded right back...

Damarr: Cool. Enjoy your day as well *winky emoji*

Getting focused, I wrote the day's lesson on the board for English and got everything ready before the kids came rushing in. By the time I was done, the bell was ringing. I took a deep breath, stood by the door to greet my kids and plastered a huge smile on my face.

Today was off to a great start...

Chapter Six

Damarr

Last night, I really enjoyed myself with Cashay. She was a very sweet girl. I could tell she had some insecurities, but hopefully, she would realize just how beautiful she was and get over all that. As confident as she tried to present herself, she allowed simple things to get to her. I wondered what had happened to her in her past to cause her to feel that way.

Me myself, I had always been secretly attracted a big boned woman. Don't get me wrong, I had experienced the thin, petite, and shapely women before, but they weren't for me. I needed a woman who wasn't fragile when I was giving her the dick. I needed a woman who ate more than a salad when we went to a restaurant. I needed a woman who didn't question me about my calories when I ordered a thick, juicy steak.

Until I met Cashay, I wasn't even looking for a relationship. I mean, I wasn't out here to find a woman, especially after just hopping out of one a couple of weeks prior. Truthfully, I didn't know what my plans were as far as staying in Houston long. All I knew was that I wasn't about to leave my family anytime soon. Ma'Dear who was the head of our family on my mother's side was taking my sister's death the hardest. Probably because she had raised Terra. Damn, my grandmother's heart had to be hurting and there she was, still standing strong while holding us all together.

Maybe I wasn't showing it on the outside, but I was torn up behind it too. Regrettably, I didn't get to spend as much time as I wanted to with Terra. She wanted to stay in Houston while I couldn't stand the sight of it after we lost our mother. Then Terra turned around and made a lot of the same mistakes that she had made.

"Talking about handing down some fucked up shit!" I thought aloud as I sat back on my bed.

As I repositioned the pillows behind me, I felt my cell vibrate. Laughing as soon as I saw the text from my 73-year-old grandmother, I opened it up and read it.

"Is she serious right now?!" I gasped. "Like I wanna hear about her and her new man! She needs to take her ass to the Senior Center and play some damn bingo or something! Talking about going out for dinner and drinks!"

Texting her back, I told her to be safe and back before the streetlights came on. Do you know this woman messaged me after that with a GIF of a hand flipping up the middle finger! My grandmother was too much!

'Suga Mama' as we called my grandmother back in Arkansas was a hot mess! Ever since her fifth husband died, she had been trying online dating! At her fucking age! I couldn't tell her shit either and neither could my cousin Erma who stayed there with her.

Arkansas was cool, but despite my well-paying job as an architect, I still managed to stay hustling in the streets. It wasn't really the dough that kept me in the game, it was the rush.

Being your own boss did something to me that made me feel powerful and accomplished at the same time. The only thing that was missing in my life was a down ass female to keep me grounded.

"Let me see what's cracking in this city," I whispered to myself as I scrolled searching for business opportunities in my field.

My plan was to get acquainted with the builders in the area then start my own company. I had high hopes that no matter where I lived, I'd be successful because I was an ambitious dude. I knew what I wanted, and I was determined.

"Okay," I sighed heavily after 30 minutes of scrolling.

As I sat up in the bed, Cashay crossed my mind. Whenever my mind idled, I just couldn't get her smile or her beautiful face out of my head. That was probably attributed by the kiss we shared last night.

Shamefully, I had kissed a lot of women in the 30 years that I had been on this earth, and that was the only one which left a sizzle on my lips. I was like damn!

Deciding to shoot her a text message before I headed out the door in search of some employment opportunities, I wanted to let her know that I was thinking about her. Even though there was some kind of history between her and my cousin Demisha, I wasn't going to let that sway me from getting to know Cashay. She was cool people so I would be a fool not to want to spend time with her.

Not sure where things were going to go with Cashay considering I lived in a totally different state, I needed to find out what her intentions were. There was no rush in asking her, but I did want to know. Finding myself going on and on in my head about where this thing was going with Cashay after only a couple of days was ridiculous.

"What the hell?" I laughed as I hopped on the highway and remembered that I was supposed to be at my grandmother's house for breakfast. Once again, I was running late, and my previous plans would have to wait.

All my older relatives got up bright and early. I was talking about the crack of dawn with the roosters and shit. When I was back home, I had a set schedule for work. Now that I was back in Houston, I had gotten laid back. It was a little harder for me to wake up as early as they wanted me to.

"Okay now!" I chanted as I arrived at my grandmother's house about 20 minutes later and got a text back from Cashay.

Sitting in the car, I exchanged messages with her until we confirmed that we would see each other later that day. Now all I had to do was figure out where I was going to take her.

"Maybe we can do something on the water since it's a nice day," I thought out loud as I got out of my car.

As I slid my cell into my pocket, I looked up and saw Demisha's raggedy car in the driveway. Maybe I shouldn't have been cracking on her whip like that because at least she had a way to transport all those kids of hers. But with all those baby daddies, she should've been collecting some type of child support so that she could be able to afford a better ride. What the hell type of dudes was she getting knocked up by anyway?

"Hey Damarr, get your butt in here!" my Uncle Terry hollered soon as my foot hit the old-fashioned foyer.

"Damarr, I didn't know you were coming!" Demisha hollered out as she ran over and hugged me.

"Yea, you know Ma'Dear can't do without her Damarr!" Auntie Dell teased playfully and moved Demisha right on out the way so that she could get her hug. The love was real, and I missed this shit.

"Where is Ma'Dear?" I asked.

"She's in the bathroom. She gon' be out in a minute. Meanwhile, y'all can go make y'all plates and have a seat in the dining room," my aunt Dell said.

When we headed to the kitchen and Demisha trailed me closely, I knew that she was going to bring up Cashay. She couldn't even wait until we got in private. Instead, she wanted act the clown that she was.

"So, cuz, you still thinking about big girl?" she asked.

"Now, here you go!" I hissed and sighed heavily. "What are you talking about Demisha?"

"You know... big girl!" she said as she opened her arms wide around her body.

"Wow!" Uncle Terry intervened and enlightened. "Yo ass just don't stop, huh? She talking about your new girlfriend Damarr. The one that she was talking about the last time."

"First of all, she's not my new girlfriend, but know that I'm not embarrassed to say that I do like this chick. I told you that yesterday Demisha. I don't know why you're so worried about me and what I'm doing or who I'm doing it with."

"I just asked a question…"

"No, you didn't just ask a question! You're being insulting and childish! I don't appreciate that either because my business is my business."

"Damn! You ain't gotta get so upset about it. It ain't even that serious," she huffed like she was offended.

"Maybe not to you, but it is to me. What you need to concentrate on are your kids and all their different daddies!" I shot just to touch enough nerve to back her up off me.

That was some bullshit right there, but I wasn't going to start no shit in my grandmother's house. The last thing I wanted was for Ma'Dear to walk in on yet another argument between the two of us. All I wanted was for my cousin to mind her damn business!

"That's how you gotta do it nephew!" Uncle Terry said.

"Whose side are you on unc?" Demisha asked.

"I'm on the right side. If you just stop picking on that man and worrying about his business, he wouldn't have to blast you."

"Who's blasting in my house?" Auntie Dell asked as her and my grandmother entered the dining room.

"Hey Ma'Dear," I said as I stood up to hug my grandmother.

"Hey baby. I'm glad you're here. Misha still giving you a hard time?" she teased with a smile.

"Nothing I can't handle," I said.

"She just misses you baby, that's all. Right Misha?" Ma'Dear asked as she looked over at my cousin.

"You're absolutely right Ma'Dear!" Demisha said with an awkward smile. "I miss him! Dassit!"

We all dug into our food talking about this, that and the other. I hoped that Demisha would let that shit with Cashay go. That was a long time ago and should be left in the past.

Now, I couldn't have her continue with this shit when I was already planning on bringing Cashay to Sunday dinner with my family. How was I supposed to do that with Demisha still acting the donkey with herself?

For all I knew, Cashay may have not liked her either! I wouldn't know that because I hadn't even revealed that Demisha was my cousin. I wondered what her reaction would be when she found out. Would that make her not want to see me again? Would that be a deal breaker for her to say, 'no way'?

To find out, I called Cashay up when I left there. She was out doing her daily walk, so I invited myself to join her since I had my sneakers on. Meeting her at a park near her house, I smiled soon as she came into view. The blue running suit that she wore hugged her in all the right spots. Her breasts, ass, hips and thighs! As thick as she was, she had a beautiful voluptuous shape.

"Hey handsome," Cashay greeted and slowed down her pace so that we could chat.

Beating around the bush, I started out by inviting her to Sunday dinner at Ma'Dear's. Cashay quickly accepted which forced me to bring up Demisha. From her reaction, I could tell it may be a problem.

"Who?!" she shrieked and stopped dead in her tracks. "That's your cousin?!"

"Yea."

"Demisha Connors is your cousin?" she questioned again.

"Yea, I know," I sighed and shook my head.

"Is she gonna be there... at Sunday dinner?"

"More than likely yes, but I know you ain't gonna let her run you off, are you?" I teased.

"You don't have to worry about her running me off. I'm worried about how I'm gonna react after the first time she says something smart to me!" Cashay snapped and explained the problems they had as kids.

"Yea, she was a bully!" I laughed.

"That shit wasn't funny then, and it ain't funny now Damarr! I'm grown and I ain't about to play those games with her childish ass!" Cashay insisted. "I might as well not go!"

"Well, I understand baby, but I really wanted you to meet my family. I've never brought nobody around them, so they're gonna know you're special."

"I am?" She giggled then frowned. "Nah, that's a set up Damarr!"

"It's not! You can hold your own and I'm gonna always have your back. If Demisha even starts, I'm gonna shut her ass up, so you don't have to worry. If she doesn't, we'll just bounce up outta there, but I know my grandmother ain't gonna have that shit. I'm her favorite and I can guarantee you that she will put Demisha out first!"

For some reason, I had a way with words and this time they were enough to sway Cashay into joining me and my family for Sunday dinner. That shit right there made my day!

Yea, flattery got me everywhere!

Chapter Seven

Demisha

The following Sunday…

It was hell on earth getting those damn kids looking nice for dinner at my grandmother's. The only reason that I was going all out was because this wasn't any old Sunday dinner. This was going to be an exciting one, with an interesting guest and I couldn't wait.

Oh, my cousin Damarr didn't think that I knew he was bringing Cashay over to Ma'Dear's. If I hadn't overheard my uncle Terry running his mouth, I would've never found out.

After discovering that the fat bitch was coming with her greedy tail, I told my auntie to make sure there was a sturdy chair to hold her big ass and plenty of food to feed the cow.

Laughing to myself, I thought back to the last time that I saw Cashay. It had to have been at least five years and she was definitely bigger than me then. I didn't know what the hell my cousin was talking about when he said that I was bigger than her!

Checking out my thickness in the floor length mirror next to the front door, I didn't think I was so big. I was 5-feet 6-inches and wore a size 16 in women's clothing. They sold that size in regular department stores, so I didn't think I was that big.

"That bitch Cashay probably at least a size 22 by now with her fat ass!" I huffed and smiled at the dress that I had to squeeze in.

Sure, the shit was uncomfortable as hell, but it sucked my damn FUPA in somewhat and made me look at least a size smaller. After having all these damn babies, it was impossible for my body to snapback to the way it used to be.

Somewhat satisfied with my appearance, I got the kids and headed over to my grandmother's house early. That way I could get the little one's situated and help prepare the meal. Homemade macaroni and cheese was my specialty and everyone's favorite.

Hopping right to it, I got all the ingredients out and prepared my dish. Since Ma'Dear had already finished her portions of the meal, I had the kitchen to myself up until Auntie Dell came meddling.

"You need to cover that up Demisha. Everybody ain't gonna be here for another hour."

"I got this auntie!" I assured and backed her off.

"Okay then!" She smirked then stared me up and down. "Why you dressed so fancy today?"

"If you wanna know... after dinner I'm going down to the new arena and get me some tickets for the grand opening next weekend. They only have limited tickets, so I gotta get there when they go on sale at 7pm. Penny is already there in line saving me a spot!"

"Can't you get them on your computer or phone or something?" Auntie Dell asked.

"Only the general admission tickets. The reserved seating you have to purchase at the place," I explained.

"That sounds expensive!"

"It is 200 a ticket, but me and Penny been saving up for the past three months for this!" I told her smiling. "Legend and his group are opening!"

"Ain't no grand opening that damn important to be paying that kind of loot for!" she fussed. "I don't care if it was Luther Vandross coming back from the dead and you know I loved me some Luther!"

"Auntie!" I laughed. "It's Legend!"

"Who the hell is that?" Uncle Terry asked coming in on the tail end of the conversation.

"Legend's real name is Lucca James. He's a guy that I used to go to school with!" I explained excitedly. I couldn't believe that someone I had gone to school with was this successful! He had groupies and everything!

"So?" Uncle Terry laughed.

"So?!" I smirked. "So, I wanna go see him perform! He's my friend!"

"If he was your friend, you wouldn't have to be standing in no long ass line, paying no damn $200 for a ticket!" Uncle Terry clowned causing me to have to lie to try to get him to shut up.

"For your information Uncle Terry, I'm going to surprise him!" I laughed. "He used to have it bad for me back in the day, so I know he's gonna be too happy to see me! Yea, he used to chase me and call me every day!"

"That was back then!" Uncle Terry cracked. "Wait until he sees you after having all them damn crumb snatchers!"

"Terry!" Auntie Dell snapped. "Cut that out! That ain't a nice thing to say! Some men like a woman with a little meat on her bones!"

"Yea, you just saying that shit because yo ass just as big as Demisha's! Both of you big..."

"You call me a bitch and you gonna have to call the law to get me up off you! Wheelchair or not!" Auntie Dell threatened.

Laughing at her, Uncle Terry wheeled his ass up out of there before my auntie made good on her word. He knew she didn't play like that!

"Anyhow, Demisha, how is the job going?" my auntie asked.

"It's going! I hate working for the state behind a damn desk! Don't worry though, I'm staying as long as somebody watches the kids for me!

"We gonna do that baby girl because you need that good paying job!"

"It's entry level auntie!" I reminded her that I had to start from the bottom.

As we conversated in the kitchen, Ma'Dear and the rest of the family came in asking to set the table. "Is it that time already?" I said out loud while wondering where the hell was my cousin Damarr and his date.

Surprised that my grandmother was going ahead on with setting the table and sitting down, I had to speak up. "We ain't waiting on Damarr grandma?"

"He's coming girl!" she said cutting her eyes. "And you betta not start no mess up in here either!"

Taking heed, I sat my ass down with everyone else. Seconds later, just like Ma'Dear said, in walked Damarr and his date.

"Hey Damarr!" all the kids hollered out as he walked by all of us and went to give our grandmother a kiss and hug.

The whole time, my eyes were stuck on Cashay who obviously had gone through some type of miracle transformation. That bitch must've had a gastric bypass or something. That made me feel some kind of way because I was looking for her to be as fat, if not fatter, than she used to be the last time I saw her.

This couldn't be the same fat bitch I used to fuck with back in the day. Not standing here like she was modeling for Fashion Nova's plus sizes!

She is still a fat bitch!

Cashay's outfit alone made me look like I shopped at the Goodwill and Damarr was right about me being bigger than her. I would never admit that shit out loud though and I definitely wasn't about to act fake and be nice to this bitch!

"So, this is the beautiful girl you told me about Damarr?" Ma'Dear went on and on about how cute Cashay was until I couldn't take it no more.

"Shit, a makeover couldn't hide her ugliness!" I cracked causing my aunt to cuss me out followed by my uncle.

Ma'Dear just sat there shaking her head. I knew she was mad, but the damage was already done.

"Didn't I tell you to behave yourself today Demisha?!" Auntie Dell huffed like she was embarrassed or some shit.

"Behave?!" I sighed. "I'm not a kid auntie! I'm grown!"

"Well hell! Act like it then! These kids of yours got more manners than you!" she hissed.

"It's okay. Demisha is obviously holding on to some ill feelings from our childhood. She's failed to realize that people grow..."

"Just like yo fat ass!" I retorted with a nasty grimace. I just knew that bitch wasn't trying to talk shit about me!

"If you don't shut your mouth Demisha, I will get up from this table and kick you out myself!" Ma'Dear threatened silencing the whole dining room. Even the kids were quiet.

"Well, you know what that means Demisha? Shut the hell up or get the hell out and don't forget yo kids!" Uncle Terry laughed.

"Terry! Another word out of you and you'll be rolled right on out with your niece! You wanna try me?!" Ma'Dear asked shaking her cane in the air. "Now, let's eat! And y'all try to act like y'all got some sense in front of our company!"

While everyone dug in, I watched as my cousin along with the rest of my family clung onto Cashay like she was a damn celebrity. That bitch was a nobody, and I would show them all soon as I got Lucca to see me.

"So, Cashay, you live around here?"

"Not too far," she replied all innocent and shit. Her sneaky ass had to have some type of skeletons in her closet and soon as I had the chance, I planned on letting them all out.

There was no fucking way on earth that I would stand by and let my cousin Damarr date that bitch! No matter how long it took, I was determined to break all that shit up just so I could get the last laugh all up in Cashay's face.

Suddenly losing my appetite, I checked the time and announced that I had to go. My auntie Dell was watching my children overnight and taking them to school in the morning, so I was about to be kid free!

Excusing myself from the table, I waited for everyone to turn around before I flipped Cashay off. Instead of lashing out at me, the bitch had the nerve to laugh! Yea, her days were numbered around here, and the clock was ticking. It was only a matter of time before I exploded on that ho!

Hugging and kissing before waving goodbye to my kids, I rushed out and hopped in my bucket and shot right down to the arena. Regretting that I didn't change the second that I got out in the heat, I was ready to cry.

Too bad I couldn't. That shit right there would make my cheap mascara run like Boston marathoners… and I couldn't have that!

I was hoping that I would get the chance to see Lucca tonight. I just knew when he saw me, he would be as happy to see me as I'd be to see him. My heart was about to burst from my chest from the excitement I was feeling. After I picked up my best friend Penny, we headed to the arena.

"Girl you excited about seeing your man?" she clowned.

"Hell yea!" I said happily.

"I can tell cuz you ain't stopped smiling since I got in the car. You keep smiling like the Joker and you gon' fuck up yo cheekbones girl!" she continued to clown me.

"Bitch hush!" I scoffed as I waved her off. "It's been so long since I've seen Lucca! Hell, I definitely haven't seen him since he became Legend!"

"Who would've thought huh? I know I never did!"

"You should've had more faith in my man than that girl! I knew Lucca would amount to something great one day!"

My mind thought back to when we were in middle school and he was crushing on me. I wouldn't give him the time of day with his lil nerdy looking ass. I wished I had taken his feelings for me more seriously instead of clowning him and making him cry.

Just the thought of the way I used to treat Lucca back then had me feeling some kind of way. I mean, what if he held a grudge against me? What if he didn't want anything to do with me? I couldn't even blame him because back then, I was an awful little kid. Everyone used to call me a bully, but I would never answer to that. I'd just beat them up!

Now that I was older, I couldn't just go around beating people up because they didn't like me or agree with me on something. I had to learn to get along with people, especially since I had kids to raise. Sure, I got food stamps and I had a decent enough place for us to stay with my Section 8 voucher. But I wanted more than that, especially for my little ones.

I didn't want them to feel they had to settle for shit to be happy. I had settled with all their daddies and now look at me. Not one of them no good niggas was around to help me take care of my brood.

I hadn't seen Josiah, Jamal's dad, since I told him I was pregnant. My son was now eight years old and had never seen his dad in person. What a fucking loser!

Jordan's dad, Jason came around when he needed a place to crash. He had a fiancée but constantly cheated on her, so on occasion she'd throw his ass out. Then he'd end up in my bed for about a week making all kinds of promises before he'd run right back to Shantelle.

Then there was Amari's daddy, Steven who didn't know if he was a boy or a man. One minute he wanted to be a family and then the next, he was gone after realizing he wasn't done chasing skirts.

Last but not least was Braegen, who was my youngest daughter Bree's dad. He was the most consistent in my bed, and the one who hurt me the most because he was the one who had my heart. I really loved Braegen, but he didn't love me. I mean, he said he did, but how could he when he treated me like shit?

He had some very good dick, which was probably why it was so hard for me to tell him no when he wanted to come over. I had never been fucked like that before. I had never felt as good with any other dude before. But I was so tired of the constant confusion I was causing my kids. I had too many different men in their lives, but I couldn't help it.

I just wanted to be happy and in love with someone.

"Hey bestie! What you over there thinking about? You and Legend?" Penny asked.

"No, just thinking."

"About what?"

Well, I certainly wasn't going to tell her about my little trip down memory lane. I didn't want to fuck up our good time by bringing up the past.

"Nothing important." I pulled into the arena parking lot and looked over at my friend.

Penny had been there for me through everything I had been through. She was the only person I trusted with my business, but I didn't want to ruin our night with my foolishness.

"You sure? Cuz you know I got your back."

"Yea, I'm sure and I know. Let's go get these tickets and hopefully, see Legend with his fine ass!" I retorted as I plastered a fake smile on my face.

"Hell yea!" Penny said. "Let's go see your man, girl!!"

I busted out laughing as we exited the car. It didn't take long once we got there for me to spot Lucca!! However, when I saw who he was with, I was ready to beat a bitch's ass!!

Chapter Eight

Katrice

It was definitely a bad idea to go with Lucca to the new area for his walk-through rehearsal. The only reason I agreed to do that shit was because I hadn't seen him in a few days due to him being out of town on business. But when we got there and saw a line wrapped around the corner, I was ready to change my mind and have him take me back home.

"What the hell?" I gasped.

"Tickets went on sale today. I didn't think they would be out here this late. It's almost six," Lucca said checking his flashy watch.

"Well, I know we're not about to fight this crowd!" I complained.

"No, we're gonna go around back to the other entrance. Security should be tight there."

See, that was just what I was talking about! Dating this man was about to be the death of me! Hell yea, I was seriously digging the way Lucca made me feel every time we were around each other. It was like nothing else even mattered.

Giving the driver specific instructions, we were pulling up at the rear entrance seconds later. "Come on," Lucca urged as he took my hand and helped me out of the car.

Holding onto me tightly, we heard someone screaming at the top of her lungs. When I looked in the direction where the voice was coming from, I saw two chicks bust through the barrier.

Rushing up to us, they were quickly stopped by Lucca's two regular guards. "Hold up! You can't be back here!"

"Wait! I just wanted to talk to Legend!" the dark- skinned chick hollered.

"Yea! My best friend used to date him! Ask him!" the tall lanky lighter girl added with her hand on her hip.

"Do you know them?" a security questioned Lucca.

"No! At least they don't look familiar!"

"It's me! It's me! Demisha!" the girl yelled bringing my eyes to hers.

Checking her out a little closer, I saw that it was indeed Demisha from our childhood. She was just as much of a bully now as she was back then.

"Demisha?" Lucca frowned and looked her up and down. "Demisha?!"

"Yea, this is me!" she sang happily. "I came to see you!"

"Okay, good seeing you again. Thanks for supporting..."

"Yes, thanks for supporting Demisha!" I added to make sure this mean big bitch knew it was me.

"Who the hell are you?"

Taking several steps towards her, I told her just who I was. "You know exactly who I am. Don't act stupid!" I told her.

When she realized who I was, boy, did that bitch's lip drop. The shit was hilarious!

"Katrice! Bony ass Katrice!" Demisha hollered as her and her friend started laughing.

"I'd hardly call this bony," I said as I showed off my assets. "But I would look bony to someone your size!" I cracked up.

"Lucca, I know you are not dating this bony ditzy ass bitch Katrice!" Demisha screamed. "No! Not that ho!"

It was funny as hell to watch her and her friend get lifted off their feet only to get thrown off the premises. The shorter guy was struggling with Demisha's big ass. Probably because that bitch had gained quite a bit of weight and in all the wrong places. She definitely didn't have any room to talk about Cashay now!

She was not going easily either. She was really putting up a fight! Hilarious!

Man! I wanted so badly to whip my phone out and record the whole scene, but I didn't want to act just as childish as her and her friend were. No, I was taught better than that.

"So, uhm, y'all used to date huh?" I clowned with a smirk as I tried to keep from laughing.

"No! Now you know I never dated Demisha!" he said as he side eyed me.

"I didn't think y'all did, but she seems to think y'all dated at some point."

"Never! We never dated!" he said with a grimace. "That whole shit was comical!"

"It really was!"

Shaking off the brief confrontation, Lucca and I were able to make it inside the arena peacefully. While he performed to an empty place, I enjoyed every moment of it.

It was when we left that my peace was disturbed. This bitch Demisha wasn't letting up. Her and her homegirl were right outside waiting on us. Where the hell was security? I had no idea!

"Didn't Cashay already cuss you out today?!" I shot.

"No, actually, I got to clown her and it's only a matter of time before my cousin kicks her to the curb. She's simply a nobody, just like you!"

"Oh, that's where you're dead wrong shorty," Lucca clowned as the driver came around and opened the car door for us. "Katrice is somebody and if you don't know it now, follow me on my social networks. I'ma make sure to let you and the rest of my fans…"

"Fan?!" Demisha snapped. "Fuck you Lucca! You wasn't nothing but a nerdy lil fucka who chased me around all through middle school!"

"Girl bye!" I huffed and waved her off.

Coming towards me full force, she raised her fist to strike me. Before Demisha's blow could connect, security showed up out of nowhere.

Seeing that I might not have another chance, I was sure to get in one good punch. Landed it dead in her mouth!

"Bitch, I told you to back up!"

Bloody lip and all, Demisha got tossed off the property again along with her stupid ass sidekick! Now, both Lucca and I were laughing.

"Can you believe that shit?!" he asked when we got into the Lincoln Town Car. "I done had plenty of chicks run up on me saying crazy shit, but for Demisha to come up here about some middle school crush..."

"Oh, so you did have a crush on her Lucca?!" I challenged looking him in the eye.

"Yea, I can admit that shit! But you remember how she was all filled out back then? She had titties and ass and all that back shit! At that age, wasn't nothing on my mind but girls and music!" Lucca laughed.

"And now?" I pressed with a smile.

"Now, it's music and one woman," he flirted as he leaned in and kissed my lips.

Day by day, this man was winning my heart. If he wasn't serenading me by phone, he was surprising me with small gifts backed by huge gestures. It was all moving so quickly that I was becoming afraid of letting myself go completely.

Protecting my heart had always been a problem because each time that I did, it was broken. I didn't think that I could take that too many more times. Celebrity or not! Lucca was no different and I planned on holding to all of my standards which included, 'no disrespect'.

So far, it was all good. Until he gave me reason to feel differently, I would tread lightly in this relationship. Watching Lucca perform on stage tonight was amazing. It was like I had a private concert just for me, and I loved every minute of it.

"What you thinking about?" he asked as he looked into my eyes.

"Your rehearsal performance earlier," I admitted.

"You liked it?"

"Hell yes! What girl wouldn't have enjoyed being serenaded by Legend? You were amazing!" I gushed. I had to catch myself because I probably sounded like one of his groupies.

"I'm glad you enjoyed it. I don't normally do rehearsal in front of an audience. It's usually just me, the sound guy and my manager."

"Well, I feel special," I confessed.

"Good. That's exactly how I want you to feel," he admitted as he leaned in for another kiss.

The kiss was light and sweet. Thank God! Had it been heated he probably would've gotten the panties right here and now!

"Whew, chile!" I gasped breathlessly as I fanned myself. That kiss was every fucking thing!

We snuggled as the driver drove me back to my place. "When can I see you again?" he asked.

"When do you wanna see me again?"

"Well, I have rehearsal all week, but if you wanna come join me that would be cool."

"I have to work all week, but maybe we can make some time for each other," I suggested.

"I always have time for you."

"I know you say that, but I don't want you to put your rehearsals aside or cut them short..."

"I would never do that. My career is very important to me Katrice. I want you to be an important factor in my life as well, but you have to understand how much I need my music."

"I do, and I'd never get in the way of that."

"With that being said, maybe after rehearsal and once you're off work, I can scoop you up and we can figure something out," he suggested.

"I'd like that," I happily replied.

"Good. Would you like me to walk you to the door?"

"I think I can do it myself but thank you. I had a great time, and I enjoyed the serenade," I reminded with a smile.

"I had a great time too," he said as he brought his lips to mine again.

This time, he added a little tongue and baby! I wondered if he could hear the gushing going on inside my panties or the fireworks going off inside my head.

After a couple of minutes, he pulled away leaving me lightheaded and a bit dizzy. My eyes were still closed until he started laughing. I finally opened them and saw the handsome smirk on his face.

"I kinda have that effect on women," he teased playfully.

"Whatever!" I scoffed as the driver opened my door. "See you soon."

"You bet you will."

As I slid out of the back seat, I stood upright and practically bounced all the way to the front door. I turned to wave before letting myself inside. After I shut the door, I leaned against it with a huge smile on my face.

Whew! That man...

Chapter Nine

Lucca aka Legend

After the driver dropped Katrice off at her place, I relaxed in the backseat and reflected on the evening. It was like a blast from the past that just kept on giving since coming back to my hometown.

Not only had I reconnected with Katrice, but then I saw Demisha who I hadn't seen since my senior year. It was so funny how I was crazy about her in middle school, but she was too much of bully to give me the time of day. I didn't really know what I saw in her back then besides her big titties and fat ass. Plus, she was always trying to clown me about the huge bifocal lenses in my frames every chance she got!

She even talked about the tape that my mother put on them when they broke too! The jokes never ended with her and the more she left me looking stupid, the more I tried to get with her like a damn dummy. I guess I thought it was better to have her as an ally than an enemy, but she wanted no parts of it. She'd rather clown me than be my friend or my girl.

Demisha wasn't the only person to clown me all the time. There were a lot of other kids that did it too.

I got called everything from Mr. Peabody the dog to Steve Urkel from *Family Matters*. I got tossed in the trashcan and had my head dumped in toilet water. When I tell you those were the worse days of my life, I meant that shit because they were.

One would think that all that harassing and hazing that I went through would make me want to quit school, but it didn't! I still had perfect attendance only because missing my music classes were not an option for me no matter how much I got bullied.

Things didn't change for me until after I graduated and went to music school in Dallas. That was where I got my swagg by growing my dreads and tossing out the glasses. It was time for me to get myself some contact lenses. That was the best decision I could've made. It was almost like once I put those contacts in my eyes, I became a totally new person!

Not only could I see the world much clearer, people could finally see the real me without the bifocals. A whole new world opened up for me then, but I never lost focus on my music. Back then, that was my only concern.

Music had always meant everything to me. It was my way to escape my real life, and through music I was able to express myself in ways I couldn't before.

Now look at me all these years later. I bet those bullies never thought I'd amount to anything, but I showed them. I proved to everyone who ever doubted me that despite how they treated me back then that I overcame it all.

"You need to stop anywhere before we make it back to your place sir?" the driver asked bringing me back to reality.

"No, I'm good. Thanks," I said as we turned into my community. "I won't need you until Tuesday. I will send you my itinerary by email tonight."

"Okay. No problem sir. I'll be here," Earl replied.

After he dropped me at my doorstep, I went straight inside and got on my computer to send my driver the information. Then I checked my notifications and found out that rehearsal for the following day was changed to that evening.

Next, I confirmed the appearance that I had to make at the high school that I graduated from. It was a special occasion because it wasn't all about me performing.

The school also asked me to speak to the kids about dreams and goals and how I got where I was today. I was honored and actually looked forward to doing that.

Teenagers were impressionable young kids. If I could help them decide what they wanted to do in the future, I was going to do it. I just wanted them to know that anything they put their minds to, could be accomplished... if they really wanted it enough and were willing to work hard for it.

Getting where I was had not been easy, but I never gave up! That was what I was sure to tell the students.

After quickly jotting down all my thoughts for my speech, I closed my computer and took my ass to sleep. My body and mind were beyond tired...

The next morning, I woke with Katrice on my mind. It was Monday morning, and I knew that she was already at work. Since I knew where her job was, I decided to surprise her with a few simple gifts.

Getting up out of my bed with a smile, I showered and sang Acapella. Loving the way that the acoustics were in the master bathroom, I let loose and ended up writing a new song in my head.

Hurrying to get dressed while I continued to hum the tune, I slid on my shoes and wrote a few notes in my musical lyrics' notebook. Once finished, I headed out to pick up some flowers, coffee and chocolates.

By now, it was nearing noon, so I had to rush to make it to Katrice's job before she left for lunch. Veering into the covered parking area a few minutes later, I lucked up on a nearby spot that a car was pulling out of.

Gathering all the gifts, I slid on my shades and made my way to the entrance. As I walked into the empty lobby area, I hurried to the information desk with my face partially covered up to conceal my identity. Waiting for this young cat to stop yapping on the phone, I finally got a chance to ask him where Katrice's office was.

"What delivery service are you from?" he questioned.

"I'm not from any delivery service!" I snapped feeling offended as I read the name on his badge. "Ryan, this is personal."

"Well, all I can tell you bruh is to leave that shit with me and I'll make sure she gets them."

"What?" I hissed.

"Yep." He laughed as though he had said something funny, but I had yet to get the joke.

As I listened to this guy tell me that he couldn't give up that info because it was against company policy, I became irritated. It made me go against the promises that I had made to myself, which was to use my clout to get my way.

Refusing to stand there looking crazy with all these gifts for one more second, I revealed my face and pulled my shades off. Everything completely changed in a single moment.

"Legend?!" he yelled sounding cool but excited.

"Hey, man! Keep that shit down! That's why I was hiding my face in the first place!" I whispered and put my shades back on.

"Man! You dating Katrice?! Katrice from the third floor? Fine ass Katrice?! Man! I've been tryna..."

"Hey dude, I just wanna surprise her and take her to lunch. Can you just call her down for me?" I asked and watched as he picked up the phone and handled my request.

Ryan's reaction made me change my mind about going to find Katrice. I could imagine how it would be if I went to her office and disrupted business with my presence.

Most of the time, I would be way more cautious when being out in public, but since I was in my hometown, I thought it would be a little different. Or so I thought.

"Legend?!" one chick hollered, and it sent off a chain reaction.

By the time Katrice came down, the lobby was filled. Regretting that I didn't bring security with me, I had to fight through the crowd to get to her.

"Lucca?! Really?!" she fussed and cut her eyes at me.

Ready to give her the gifts that I brought for her to use as a valid excuse was useless. The box of chocolates had been smashed up, the flowerless stems was all that was left of the floral arrangement and the coffee had spilled all over my clothes.

"You tried, huh?" Katrice teased and grabbed me by the hand to lead me out the back while the company security held the crowd back.

"Yes! I swear I tried! I never thought it would be anything like that!" I confessed feeling bad about it all.

"You know that now I'm never gonna get a moment of peace at my job, right?" she fussed as we walked around to her car and got in before someone spotted us.

Taking the back exit out of the employee lot, Katrice laughed and hit my thigh. "I can't believe you Lucca!"

"What?!" I cracked with a smile. "I just wanted to see you!"

"I thought we decided to hook up AFTER work today?!"

"I forgot that rehearsal wasn't until tomorrow because I gotta get ready for this thing up at our old high school."

"What?!" she shrieked. "I wanna go! I would love to see some of my old teachers!"

"I would've invited you, but it's tomorrow during the day. I just thought you would probably have to work."

"Hold on!" she said hopping on her cell to call her boss.

The whole conversation, Katrice was giggling. When she got off, she looked at me and busted out laughing.

"What?" I asked.

"I guess it wasn't all bad that you came to my job today and created total chaos!"

"Why you say that?"

"Because my boss was so excited to know that I knew you that she not only gave me the day off, she gave me the entire week off!" She laughed. "The only catch is that I had to promise her an autographed photo of you."

"Oh, is that all?!" I replied with a smile. "I got a bunch of that shit at the house! Since you're off for the rest of the week starting now, why don't we go by there and get it?"

"Huh?"

"Huh?" I mocked Katrice playfully. "Come on now! I done been to your crib at least three times and you ain't been to mine once."

"I know but..."

"Look, if you don't feel comfortable when we get there, you can stay in the car while I go inside and get the picture."

"If we get there and find no fans or crazy folks hanging around, then I might come in!" she responded with a smile as her cell rang. "This is Cashay. Let me take it right quick!"

As Katrice talked to her friend and told her about what happened, I laughed at how dramatic she was. It was cute and she was amazing. Now, if I could just get her inside my house...

Chapter Ten

Cashay

"So, you're finally going over to his house huh?!" I screamed excitedly. It was about time Katrice got her some business of her own so that she could stay out of mine!

Mad love was what I had for my best friend, but she had been acting up lately. The only thing that made her smile these days was the mention of Lucca's name! In that case, I would be screaming it from the hilltops if it was going to make my bestie happy.

"Yes! I might just go inside. Who knows?!" Katrice giggled. "But how are you calling me right now? You're on lunch?"

"Girl, I told you last week that we went on spring break starting today! No lil kids for the next seven days!"

"Oh, yea! That's right!" she replied. "Enjoy your vacation sis and I pray you don't have any more run ins with that Demisha! Lord knows that the one night I had to deal with her was more than enough! That chick is straight crazy!"

"Yes, she is!" I laughed and wrapped up our call as soon as I saw Damarr ringing my other line.

Quickly answering it, the first thing he asked me was where I was at. "Now you know that I'm on vacation this week!"

"That's right!" Damarr laughed.

"What's up with you?" I asked.

"Nothing much. Was just thinking about you. Wanted to know if I could see you today. I know after the ghetto ass scene at my grandmother's yesterday, you might need a break. If you do, I totally understand that shit. Demisha is a fucking character..."

"We've already discussed this, and I told you Damarr! That girl ain't nothing but a bunch of bark and I wasn't about to punch her lights out in your grandmother's house. Now, cousin or not, if she tries that shit in the streets, I'm gonna lay that ass out!" I assured causing him to laugh loudly.

"Stop that Cashay!" he continued to tease.

"What's so funny?"

"You are so sweet and you're a schoolteacher! Then there's another side of you! It's one to be reckoned with too!" he clowned.

"Are you talking about me Damarr?!" I questioned starting to feel offended.

"Hell yea! I'm talking the truth and I'm attracted to all of it! The good, the bad and the beautiful because there ain't no ugly when it comes to you baby," he wooed making me let my guards back down.

"Okay, so you're not being mean huh?" I giggled.

"I could never see myself being mean to you baby," he replied sounding all sexy and shit.

"I hope not!" I joked. "So, what are you doing today?"

"I just got this contract to draw up the drafts for a new building going up downtown. I put the bid in yesterday and was shocked when I got that shit!"

"What?!" I screamed happily. "That's so good Damarr! I'm so happy for you! Congrats!"

"Thanks!" he replied. "You wanna hook up later so that we can celebrate?"

"Yea! For sure! What did you have in mind? And please don't say dinner at your grandmother's! Not to be funny because they all seemed cool as hell. It's just that one who rubs me the wrong way!"

"Okay, okay! You got me! I'm not gonna take you nowhere around where she'll be. At least I'll try not to! When it comes to Demisha, you never know what she might do and where she might be because her ass be popping up everywhere!" he clowned.

"Well, if she pops up around me, just know that she's gonna get popped!" I laughed.

"Here you go!" he cracked. "Just come to my house tonight around five. I'll have everything set up and we can eat there."

"Oh, an intimate celebration huh?" I giggled wondering what I should wear for such a special occasion.

Since we hadn't gone all the way, I wanted to be ready just in case tonight would be the night. Getting excited, I hung up with Damarr with butterflies dancing in my stomach.

No man had ever treated me so nicely. The way that he always went above and beyond to make me feel special meant so much to me. All I wanted to do was show him just how much.

"It's one already! That only gives me a few hours to get ready!"

Frantically hopping up from the sofa, I stripped out of my loungewear and tried on everything in my closet that still had tags on them. That took me an hour alone!

Finding the perfect dress that would hide the sexy black lingerie beneath, I laid it out with a new pair of black platforms that I had purchased a month back. After hopping in the shower to freshen up, I washed my hair to make my natural curls pop.

By the time I finished pampering myself, it was nearly 4pm. That meant that I needed to get going. Rushing out to hop in the car, I got halfway to Damarr's and realized that I didn't have anything to bring.

Since it was a celebration and we were having an intimate dinner at his home, I could at least stop and get a bottle of wine and a card. Swinging by the local HEB, I hurried inside and went to the back where they kept the alcohol.

Not watching where I was walking, I ran right into a display of Nestle Quik boxes. "Fuck!" I fussed as I squatted carefully to pick them up.

"Let me help you get that," a male voice offered.

"Thanks. I can't believe how clumsy I can be sometimes!" I admitted as I stood upright and turned to face the guy.

"Cashay?!" Tay questioned raising his brow.

"Tay?!" I screamed as I jumped in his arms and hugged him. "Is that really you?"

"In the flesh girl!"

"Damn! Katrice didn't tell me that you were gonna be in town!"

"Probably because she doesn't know it yet. I'm just in the states for a couple of weeks to train some people on intake at the Houston MEPS base. Then it's back to Hawaii."

"Oh my God! Is that where you live now?! I thought you were in North Carolina?" I asked.

"Yea, I was there and a bunch of other places, but I'm doing my last tour on Oahu!" He laughed as he looked me up and down. "Damn! You done grown up on me huh?"

"Well, I know you didn't think I'd stay that little fat kid forever, did you?" I blushed.

"Nah, I didn't. You are just as beautiful as ever though!"

"And just as big as ever too!" I laughed thinking back to when I used to get teased.

"Stop it! You are fine as fuck and don't let nobody tell you different!"

Okay, now he was making me blush like a little kid. I remembered how Tay, Katrice's cousin used to stand up for me all the time when we were younger. That was one thing I really liked about him. He always took my side against the bullies, mostly Demisha's crazy ass! I hadn't seen Tay in years and neither had Katrice. I knew that she would be happy when she found out he was back in Houston.

"So, did you just get here?" I asked wondering why he hadn't contacted Katrice yet.

"Yea, I got in this morning. Checked into my hotel then called your mother, Gena to get you guys' address."

"You talked to my mother?!" I shouted and felt bad that I hadn't spoken to her much lately. Maybe if I had, I would've known that Tay was coming to town. Damn! What else was she keeping from me?

Tossing my thoughts to the side, I listened as Tay told me that he had been sending money to my mother while we were growing up. I didn't know if Katrice knew, but I had no idea.

"What are you all dressed up for and please don't tell me that somebody done snatched you up already!" Tay teased as he lifted my left hand and noticed that I wasn't wearing a ring. "No ring might give a brutha some hope!"

"Huh?" I laughed. "Stop playing Tay! We're just like family! Katrice is like my sister, so..."

"So, you look at me like a cousin or some shit?" he asked with a serious expression.

Even as fine and established as Tay was, I didn't see him in that way. He was nearly seven years older than me, and I wasn't at all interested, but I didn't want to hurt his feelings.

"Not like that Tay! Now maybe if you would've come home a month or two ago, I might have considered looking at you differently, but now, I have my eye on someone special."

"So, that's where you're going all dressed up huh?" he asked. I couldn't help but notice a twinge of disappointment in his facial expression.

"Yea, and I need to get going before I'm late!" I smiled and gave him one last hug.

He held me just a tad bit longer and a whole lot closer than I expected. The sweet scent of his cologne and manliness had me feeling a little lightheaded. I gently pulled from his embrace and tried to quickly regain my composure.

Grabbing a couple of different brands of wine, I breezed through the self-checkout line and ran to my car. Once I was inside, I cracked up and called Katrice to see if she was still with Lucca.

"Girl! I know it's supposed to be a surprise but…"

"I know! I'm talking to Tay on the other line right now!" She laughed excitedly. "I'm going to the house to meet up with him! Meet us there!" Katrice cheered.

"I'll be there later. You two enjoy some quality time together and after dinner with Damarr, I'll be home. Or maybe I won't be!"

"You nasty girl you!" Katrice laughed. "You better get you some and get your ass back home tonight! Tay really wants to see you!"

"Yea, what's up with all that?"

"Girl! I don't know! But the way he just called me and sweated me about you!" She giggled like it was the funniest thing.

Well, it wasn't, and I was already involved with Damarr. The last thing I needed was Katrice playing matchmaker right now!

The LAST thing!

Chapter Eleven

Damarr

Man! I had everything set up perfectly a whole hour before Cashay was supposed to arrive. Ordering food, flowers and candles online was the business. I didn't have to leave the house to create an ambience that would bring even the holiest virgin out of her panties!

Hearing a sudden pounding at my front door caused me to check the time again because I wasn't expecting Cashay for another hour. Before rushing anxiously to answer it, I got my cell and checked for missed calls and texts.

"Fuck!" I whispered.

There were ten missed calls and several unopened text messages. Most of them were from my family members, including Demisha.

As I opened the first text, the beating at my door got louder. Tossing my cell to the side, I went stomping angrily to see who was knocking like that.

Swinging the door open with a major attitude, it only got worse when I saw my cousin Demisha standing there. Instead of letting me invite her in, she brushed right by me and started fussing.

"You ain't hear us calling you for the past two hours?!" Demisha snapped.

"Is Ma'Dear okay?"

"Yes! She's okay, Uncle Terry is okay, Auntie Dell is okay..."

"Well, what the fuck is the emergency?" I questioned as Demisha wandered her ass right into the den.

"I guess nothing! Shit! You don't wanna hear what I gotta say and let it ruin this night you have planned!" she clowned and then frowned. "Please don't tell me you're doing all this shit for Cashay's fat ass! If you are, you definitely don't have enough food here for her!"

As she went to dip her finger into the chicken strips, I slapped it away and backed her ass right on up. "What did you come over here for Demisha? Just tell me and get to stepping! I got company coming over and I'm not about to have you here when she gets here!"

"When who gets here? Huh? Who's coming here?" Demisha persisted. "Please say anybody else but Cashay's big bucket ass!"

"I told you to watch what you say about her!" I warned.

"I'm not gonna apologize for it."

"Maybe not, but you will respect her."

"What is it that you see in her anyway?" she asked.

"If you weren't such a bully, you might be able to see the good in her too!" I countered. "Now, if you'll excuse me!"

"Okay, I'll leave. But just know that your grandmother on yo daddy's side called down here and said that some chick named Chandra came over there and busted all the windows out of the two cars you left over there!"

"What the fuck?!" I hissed not ready to deal with any of the bullshit that Demisha was telling me. "It's not like I can do shit about it while I'm way in Houston!"

"Well, maybe you can because from what she told Ma'Dear, the chick said she'll be here soon!"

"She doesn't know where I live!"

"That ain't what I understood!" Demisha said.

"Well, what do you understand? I mean, how would she know where I live?"

"She played the hell out of Suga Mama and got all the information that she needed. Made her think that she was having your baby and she was coming to surprise you!" Demisha laughed. "So, I'm gonna go and let you enjoy your dinner. Just remember to watch your back because this Chandra chick could show up any day! Shit, you be calling me crazy, but that chick sounds like she got hella screws loose!"

"Get out Demisha!"

Snatching up a couple of pieces of chicken, she flew out the door laughing loudly. That shit burned me up, but I didn't have time to entertain it. Cashay would be here any minute now. And just as I suspected, as soon as Demisha pulled off in that old bomb, Cashay pulled up.

I was already standing in the doorway, so I just walked out to meet her. I opened the door for her, and the fragrance of her perfume almost knocked me off my feet. She stepped out looking like a million bucks and I had to restrain myself.

I kissed her on the cheek and said, "Damn! You look amazing!"

"Thank you," she said with a shy smile. "Uhm, I just saw your cousin down the road. Is she coming back?"

"Hell nah! She had dropped by to see if I cooked. You know her ass is greedy!" I commented. The last thing I wanted to discuss was my ex back home who might be coming to invade my present life here.

Once Cashay left, I was going to have to give my grandmother a call and get my windows fixed. But for right now, all I wanted to concentrate on was this beautiful thick ass female in my presence.

"Thank God!" she enthused. "I bought some wine."

I opened the back door and retrieved the wine she had purchased. I shut the door and we headed inside the house hand in hand.

"Damn, you smell good! What's say we skip dinner and go right to dessert?" I flirted. She giggled and her cheeks reddened as she blushed.

"Boy you better stop!" she said, probably thinking that I was joking. I really wasn't and if I wasn't such a gentleman, I would show her just how serious I was.

"I hope you brought your appetite," I said.

"You know I can eat," she joked. "Babe please tell me you cooked more than just chicken strips."

"These ain't just any chicken strips now! These are my famous garlic parm chicken strips to go with my famous spaghetti and meatballs. I also made a Cesar salad and French bread."

"Wow babe! You went all out for a girl!" she gushed.

"Not just any girl," I said as I closed the space between us. "MY girl."

Tilting her chin upward, I planted a soft and sensual kiss on her lips. Once our lips parted, she released an exasperated breath.

"Whew! Well, alrighty then!"

"There's plenty more where that came from."

"Well, say that then!" she gasped as I released her.

"If you'll have a seat in the dining room, I'll get the rest of this spread on the table."

"Do you need any help? I can bring something or at least pour the wine," she offered with a huge smile.

"Well, you can get the salad out the fridge, and I also have a bottle of Moscato chilling in there if you wanna grab that too," I suggested.

"Will do." She opened the fridge and placed the bottles of wine she purchased in and took the chilled one out along with the salad and dressing. I followed behind her with the chicken, spaghetti and French bread.

"Oh my God babe! These flowers are gorgeous!"

"Not as gorgeous as you are," I said.

"Okay, you know what?" she asked as she removed her dress and stood there in her lingerie. "I was gonna wait until later, but maybe we should have that dessert now. I mean right now!"

"Huh?" I wanted to make sure that I understood her correctly before I pulled out my big gun.

"You heard me zaddy! Come and get it!"

Shit, that was all she had to say...

Chapter Twelve

Tay

Damn! Seeing Cashay had me feeling some kind of way. I hadn't expected that when I stopped at HEB for some wine. I had the address of where her and my cousin lived, so I didn't want to go by there empty handed. Which was what I was doing in the store... picking up a bottle of wine. You could imagine my surprise when I saw Cashay bent over picking up some shit she dropped to the floor.

Hell, all I saw was her backside, but I'd recognize that booty anywhere. I was surprised that she wasn't married or engaged by now, and even though she said there was someone special in her life, I didn't care. The fact that she didn't have a ring on her finger made her fair game. Holding her fluffy ass in my arms definitely had me feeling some kind of way.

She smelled so good that I didn't want to let her go. Now, I didn't want anyone thinking I was some pervert after a little kid because I wasn't. I was only a few years older than she was and we were both grown. It wasn't like I was the same age

I was back when I was saving her from Demisha's ass.

After we said our goodbyes, I headed to the checkout counter and then to see my cousin Katrice. I hit her up on the way to let her know that I had seen Cashay in the store.

"Hey Tay!" she greeted happily.

"Hey cuz. What you got going on?" I asked.

"Nothing much. What about you?"

"Well, I'm in town so I thought..."

She started screaming before I could finish what I was saying. "Are you serious right now? You're in Houston?"

"I am. I actually just ran into your girl at the HEB," I said.

"Who? Cashay?"

"Yep. Damn she looks good as fuck!"

"Boy stop!"

"I'm serious! She mentioned that she was seeing someone."

"She is."

"Is it serious?" I inquired.

"I'm not sure. They just started dating…"

"Then it can't be that serious," I remarked. "She mentioned that she was going on a date. I'm headed to your place. Do you think she'll be back tonight?"

"I have no idea, but you're definitely welcome to come chill! I can't believe you're in town!"

"I am. I can't believe Cashay looks the way she does."

"And she's beeping my other line. Hold up a minute." She clicked the line and was gone for a couple of minutes. "I'm back."

"Look I'll be pulling up to your place in about five minutes," I informed her.

"Good. I can't wait to see you."

"Me either, cuz. It's been a long time."

"Too long."

We ended the call and I smiled at the thought of seeing my cousin after all this time. I pulled into the driveway of a really nice house a few minutes later. I got the wine and headed to the door. Katrice rushed out and jumped in my arms before I had a chance to knock or ring the bell.

"Oh my God!" she cried as she jumped into my arms. "I can't believe you're here!!"

I hugged her as I smiled. I couldn't believe I was here either. It had been at least 10 years since I had last seen my cousin. She dragged me inside the house and stood there staring at me for at least five minutes with tears in her eyes.

"What's wrong? I got some shit on my face or something?" I asked.

She busted out laughing as I used my hand to rub down my face. The way she was looking at me, I wanted to make sure my face wasn't dirty.

"No, silly! I'm just so happy to see you. You look great in that uniform," she said.

"Thanks, cuz. A couple of women who tried to hit on me earlier said the exact same thing." I chuckled as I remembered the two women in HEB who were practically throwing themselves at me.

"I can only imagine. Come sit with me."

After I followed her into the den, we started talking about everything. When she mentioned that Lucca was in town and how he had blown up as Legend, I was shocked. Not too shocked though because I remembered how much he liked music as a kid. What I was shocked about the most was when she told me they were dating.

"You dating Lucca Urkel?" I asked in surprise.

"Please don't call him that! He has changed a lot since then. I barely recognized him when I first saw him," she admitted.

"Well, if you like him and he makes you happy, I love him. So, what's up with your girl?"

"Who... Cashay?"

"Well, I sure wasn't talking about Demisha's ass?" I responded as we both cracked up laughing.

"You know Demisha is in the market for a new man," she replied.

"I am not about to play with you," I retorted as I shot her a dirty look.

"Sorry cuz, but you kinda had that coming."

"Whatever. Back to the question. What's up with Cashay?" I asked. "Since you need me to be more specific."

"Well, she's working as a schoolteacher at Cinco Ranch Junior High, and she just started seeing someone. What's up with your sudden interest in her?"

"Well, I saw her earlier and was surprised by how much I was feeling her. I didn't expect to feel that way."

"So, you're smitten?"

"If that's what you wanna call it. I just know that I wanna know more about her and spend some time with her while I'm here."

"Does she know you're feeling her like that?"

"I flirted with her a little in the store, but I'm not sure she took me seriously," I admitted.

"Well, there's nothing I would love more than to see my best friend and cousin together."

"Really?"

"Hell yea! I trust you more than anybody, so the two of you together would be great!"

"So, will you help me out?" I asked.

"Help you out with what?"

"Operation Steal Cashay!"

Katrice busted out laughing and so did I. I guess that shit did sound funny, but I was dead serious. I was here for two weeks and I wanted to spend as much time with Cashay as possible.

"Operation Steal Cashay? Really Tay!"

"That's the whole plan in a nutshell. I just want the chance to spend some time with her. If shit between her and ol' boy ain't serious like that, it shouldn't be too hard for me to wrangle her away," I reasoned.

"Well, I'll do my best to help you in any way that I can. Cashay deserves to be with someone as honorable as you. Hell, you're out there serving our country. The least she can do is spend some time with you."

"I hope she does."

"What's say we go to dinner and hatch a plan for you to steal Cashay?" she offered.

"Sure thing."

So, we left the house and went out to eat. I was in the mood for seafood, so we decided to go to Krab Kingz in Cypress. Over dinner and King

Crabs we discussed how she would help me get with Cashay. I just hoped the plan worked.

Chapter Thirteen

Katrice

All through dinner, my cousin Tay bugged me about Cashay. I didn't know what the sudden attraction to her was and every time that I asked him, he gave me some lame ass excuse.

"So, you wanna tell me about this crazy crush that you have for my homegirl all of a sudden?!" I asked smiling at how handsome he looked in his uniform. He wanted to change before we left to eat, but I begged him to leave it on because I was so proud of him.

"Katrice, I told you. I didn't expect these feelings either. It's just that when I saw her, it caught me by surprise. Hell, I never looked at her like that because back then, all y'all were kids to me. Now that we're grown, I see Cashay in a whole different way cuz! Truthfully, Katrice, it's her thickness for me!"

"Here you go Tay!"

"No! I'm so serious Katrice and I'm gonna holla at her first chance I get. I hope she's home when we get back to your place," he replied. "I got that hotel room, but I don't wanna go back there alone."

"So, you think you're gonna sweep Cashay off her feet fast enough to get her to go to your hotel room with you Tay?!" I shrieked and shook my head. "That's my homegirl and she's like my sister, boy! If all you want is a piece of ass, I do believe Demisha is still single!"

"Here you go with that bullshit, cousin!" Tay laughed. "If she was the last chick on earth, I'd spend my last day jacking off!"

"You are so stupid!" I laughed as we headed out of the restaurant.

The entire ride home, all Tay wanted to talk about was Cashay. It made me think that he was just getting out of a bad relationship or something. My nosy ass had to start prying.

"So, you ain't got no girl in Hawaii?" I pressed.

"Nah, I dated this one chick Aolani, but she was too clingy and shit. Wanted to make me follow all of their traditions and was too against things I liked to do."

"How long y'all been broke up?"

"Me and Aolani split up last year. I've been dating casually since then, but no one has been able to spark something in me until today. As soon as I laid eyes on Cashay, it was like seeing her lit a fire or something inside of me. I like that feeling and I'm wanna explore that shit. I don't give a damn about some young nigga she's seeing. Me and her have history..."

"Please Tay! You babysat us a few times and took us to the store and shit! That's all the history y'all got!" I reminded him as I shook my head at him. He was too funny.

"You know what I mean Katrice. I've been knowing Cashay practically her whole life! That's gotta count for something! Shit! You let that corny ass nigga Lucca back in your life after not seeing him for years! Why can't I get that same shot with your homegirl?"

Tay was right and at that moment, I had nothing to come back at him with. The only thing that I could do was laugh at his crazy ass.

"We'll see Tay!"

"You think she's coming home tonight?" he asked as we made it back to my place.

"Well, she usually comes home every night, but like I said Tay, Cashay just started dating this dude. I don't know how serious they are to be honest."

"So, she ain't never spent the night with old boy?"

"Don't get your hopes up cousin! It's already getting late and she's not here yet!" I teased and got him out a blanket and pillow. "Here, since you're gonna wait for her!"

"Hush! Stop making it seem like I'm sweating her or some shit Katrice. I just wanna spend some time with her and see where it goes from there," he tried to convince me.

"You go ahead and figure that shit out cousin! I'm going to bed! I got the 'itis'!" I laughed and retreated to my bedroom.

After changing into some pjs, I got in the bed and sent Cashay a text to see if she planned on coming home tonight. Of course, I left out the part about Tay being on the sofa waiting for her. That was going to have to be a surprise for her to receive once she did make it back to the house.

Scrolling Facebook, I stayed up another hour to see if Cashay would reply to my text. When she didn't, I gave up and went to sleep.

Man, I was in a deep slumber too and was having the best dream ever about Lucca until Cashay came busting in my room when it was still dark out.

"Katrice! Katrice!" she whispered while shaking my body.

"What?! What the hell is it?!" I snapped and rubbed my eyes so that I could see the time clearly on the digital clock that sat on the nightstand next to my bed. "5:00 in the morning?! Are you just getting here?"

"Yes! Now what I need you to do is tell me what Tay is doing here! He told me that he got a hotel room! He scared the shit out of me!"

"Sorry about that, but I did text you last night. If you had responded..." She rolled her eyes upward. "Anyway, he does have a hotel room. But we went to dinner last night and we were drinking..."

"Oh, okay," she said as her facial expressions softened.

"What's wrong with you? You just now getting home?"

"Yea!" she whispered with a wide grin as she got up and closed my bedroom door so that she could tell me all about her finally giving Damarr some of her goodies.

As happy as I was for her, I couldn't help but to feel bad for my cousin Tay. He had gotten his hopes up so high that I couldn't be the one to burst his bubble. Instead, I just gave Cashay a big hug and told her to go wash her ass.

"Shut up!" she teased as she went for the door. Turning back around to me, she smiled and told me how good it was to her before switching her big hips out my room. That girl was too much!

Now feeling anxious about what to say to Tay, I got up and freshened up then went out to the kitchen to cook some breakfast. While I cut up some red potatoes and stuck some biscuits in the oven, I got a pack of thick cut pepper bacon out of the fridge. Just as I turned around, Tay scared the shit out of me by sneaking up behind me.

"My badd Katrice!" He laughed with his breath smelling like toothpaste and mouthwash. "I didn't mean to scare you!"

"I didn't even hear you get up!" I replied and punched him playfully. "Cashay up yet?"

"She's here?!" he asked as he anxiously looked around.

"Yea, she's here," I answered without giving him any specifics like the time she came in or what she had been out doing. It was none of my damn business and at this point, I was ready to stay out of it.

Only thing was, Tay wasn't about to let me. He was already in my face asking me a million questions about what Cashay liked, what her interests were, her favorite color, what music she listened to. It was all so overwhelming, and I got no relief until Cashay finally waltzed her ass in the kitchen a half hour later... just when I finished cooking. There the three of us were, up and ready to eat when it was barely 6:00 in the morning.

"Good morning beautiful!" Tay greeted Cashay, which caused her to blush like a schoolgirl. It was so cute!

"Hey Tay! What you still doing here? I thought for sure you would've hooked up with one of your old freaks by now," she teased.

"Girl, my days of fucking with freaks been behind me. The only chick I was trying to reunite with ain't tryna give a brutha no play."

Shut Cashay's ass right on up. She was clearly stumped because she didn't say another word.

"Oh, I guess that ain't what she wanted to hear," he smirked in disappointment.

"Tay, stop playing so much! I told you that I'm seeing somebody..."

"So, do that mean you can't have friends? I mean, you did say we were practically family. Just tell him that I'm back in town and you're gonna spend some time with me. That way, you won't be lying!"

"Yea, that's true Cashay!" I added as I took a bite of my crunchy bacon.

Before she had a chance to respond, her cell began to ring. After checking her screen, she excused herself with a look that spelled trouble.

Running behind her, I waited for the chance to ask some questions while I eavesdropped on her conversation with Damarr. All I could get out of the whole thing was some shit about this bitch Chandra who he used to mess with.

Supposedly, this chick was the one who busted out his car windows. I didn't know how much more there was to this story, but from what I heard, it didn't sound good.

Not good at all!

Chapter Fourteen

Demisha

It took me almost a whole day to get Chandra's number from my grandmother and I had to sneak it out of her phone at that! I hated to be so fucking scandalous and get it like that, but I needed to get this chick to Houston to bust up this shit between Damarr and Cashay. There was no way I was going to let that fat bitch get my cousin fall any deeper for her big fake and phony ass.

Dialing Chandra up the next morning, she answered on the first ring thinking that I was Damarr. "Why the fuck you just calling me back now? I been left messages for your ass!"

"Ah, this is Demisha, Damarr's cousin," I introduced.

"Is he okay?" she asked sounding panicked.

"Yea, he's good, but I thought that I would drop a gem on you before you came out here to Texas."

"What's up?" Chandra questioned.

"Well, I'll just come out and say it. He's fucking with another chick out here," I revealed. "I know you're having his baby, so I thought that you needed to know what was going on here so you wouldn't step into a pile of shit soon as you got off the plane."

"He's what?!"

"He got himself a girlfriend out here... a big fat one too!" I clowned.

"Oh, hell nah! Damarr got me fucked up if he thinks I'm gonna continue playing these childish ass games with him."

"I don't blame you girl!" I laughed to myself. "Oh but, let me warn you that Damarr is heated that his grandmother gave up his info to you."

"As much as I like Suga Mama, I'm tired of her protecting Damarr's ass like he's a baby. I didn't intend to go over there and be disrespectful, but when she wouldn't tell me what I needed to know and I saw his cars just sitting there, I couldn't stop myself from reacting. There was nothing that could stop me from busting out those damn windows. Sure, I got the info from her after acting crazy, but it didn't make me feel better though and now that you done told me all this, I can't get there soon enough!" Chandra fussed. "If it wasn't for me telling her that I was pregnant and bursting in tears right there in front of her, Suga Mama was gonna call the cops on me! I'm so glad she didn't because then I was gonna have to really act a damn fool!"

This chick seemed like she was seriously in love with my cousin Damarr and from the sounds of things, she was crazy as hell. Chandra proved that shit by vandalizing his cars right in front of his grandmother.

Pregnant or not, if that had been Ma'Dear, she would've been out there with a damn broom beating the hell out of her ass! Chandra had gotten lucky there in Arkansas and now I was about to make her even luckier! I was about to be her lifeline to fuck this bitch Cashay up! Little did she know, I was about to use her ass until I used her up.

If she lost the baby or got locked up, that was on her. All I was worried about was getting Cashay away from my cousin. Nothing more.

"I'm coming though! I just don't know where to go once I get there. I have your grandmother Ma'Dear's address, but Suga Mama said Damarr wasn't staying there."

"No, he has his own place. I'll give you my address and you can come here first. Then I will call and see where Damarr is," I suggested like I had it all planned out.

"Cool, I'm coming."

"How long does it take you to get here from Arkansas?" I inquired.

"I ain't got time to be booking no last-minute airlines ticket, so to get there quicker, I'm gonna have to drive."

"How long does that take!?" I sighed ready for her to get her ass to Houston to beat Cashay's ass.

"According to the Google map, it will take me almost seven hours to get from Little Rock to Houston," Chandra told me.

She was dumb as fuck if you asked me. How the hell would a seven-hour drive be quicker than a two-hour plane ride? That ho' didn't have the good sense God gave her if she couldn't do simple addition. No wonder my cousin liked her simple ass.

"That's not soon enough because I'm anxious to get in Damarr's face to let him know that I'm not playing with him! How dare he change his damn number and didn't bother giving me the new one! I guess he thought if I couldn't contact him, I'd let shit go. But he should've known better."

"You know how sneaky niggas can be!" I laughed as I touched on a nerve.

"Yea, I do, but the audacity of your cousin though!" Chandra huffed. "How the hell did he think he could just say it was over and it would be over? We have been in a relationship for three fucking years! If he wasn't willing to fight for us, he should've just said that shit! That's okay though because the last thing I'm doing is giving up. I still love Damarr and that's all we need to make this work! Well, love and trust."

"So, why did y'all break up?"

"Shit, I don't know! All I knew was that he was going to Houston for his sister's funeral. Next thing I knew, he was gone and all his shit was too! It was like he abandoned me without notice! How he gonna just do some shit like that when I'm carrying his baby?"

"That's fucked up!" I said even though what this chick Chandra was telling me sounded like a bunch of bull. Honestly, I was starting to doubt that she was pregnant at all. That was something I would have to see for myself once she got to Houston.

"It's all messed up, Demisha!" Chandra sighed heavily. "This time, flowers, candy and gifts are not gonna make it better! Damarr has to grow up!"

Maybe Chandra was right, but I wasn't my cousin's mama, and he was grown as far as I was concerned. This bitch I was talking to sounded more and more like a fucking mental patient that had it bad for my cousin!

What I was getting myself into, I didn't know. But if it was going to split Damarr and Cashay up, I was with all the shit!

"Let me get off of this phone Demisha. Thank you so much for reaching out to me. I don't know what I would've done if you hadn't." She laughed. "Probably showed up over at your grandmother's and acted a fool!"

"Well, be glad that you didn't Chandra because Ma'Dear ain't nothing like Suga Mama! She don't play that shit and she got a gun she ain't afraid to use either! Yep, she definitely would've popped you a hot one all up and through yo ass!" I warned.

The last thing that this deranged chick wanted was smoke from my family. We were all a little touched when it came to the bullshit.

"You crazy girl! I like you already!" She giggled like I was joking with her. "I'll call you and check in while I'm on the road. I'll be leaving within the next hour or so."

"Okay girl! Be safe!" I told her then hung up and busted out laughing.

It was about to be drama at its finest and I couldn't wait to meet this Chandra girl in person. If she was any kind of crazy like she seemed to be, I was about to be in a world of trouble.

"Well, I like trouble and trouble ain't never stopped me from doing shit before!" I said to myself in the mirror.

It was day three of my Keto diet and I was about to go crazy with no sugar, potatoes, pasta and bread! I had already lost a few pounds and that was the only reason why I kept going. I was going to get this weight off of me just so I could clown Cashay and Damarr for clowning me about my size.

Back in the day, I used to be the shit! I had the best body out of all the girls my age. That was just how I kept getting knocked up!

Now that my tubes were tied and no more babies were coming out of this coochie, I needed to get myself together! Physically fit at the least.

After taking care of everything for the day, I checked the clock as there was a knock on my door.

"Damn, time flies!" I gasped as I opened it up to see this chick Chandra standing there in designer shit from head to toe. She had on so much jewelry I thought the bitch was gonna fall over.

"Demisha?" she questioned frowning up as she stepped inside my apartment.

Here I was trying to help my cousin Damarr with his personal life since he was doing such a lousy job, and I got literally no thanks whatsoever. From the moment that bougie bitch Chandra walked into my apartment, she had her nose in the damn air. Just thinking about her reaction to my place made me wanna snatch that tacky ass weave out of her head.

Well, to me it was tacky, but that bitch had her hair laid! I was a bit jealous to be honest, but I'd never confess that shit to her.

"Eww! Is this where you really live?" she asked as she walked in. "Oh God! It's even worse on the inside! And what's that smell?"

She scrunched her nose up like she had never smelled a place where kids lived. I mean, I may have needed to wash the dishes and clothes, but my apartment didn't smell that funky! This bitch was seriously overdramatic!

"Girl it really stinks in here!"

Man, I looked at her like she was losing her fucking mind. This bitch didn't know me to be talking to me like that. My apartment might not be much to some, but it was home to me and my kids. And it was affordable for me.

Like where the fuck did she get off judging me when I was out here trying to help her fucking ass?! The nerve of this bitch!

"Uh, excuse you!" I said as I closed the door behind her.

"I'm sorry, but how long is it going to take for Damarr to get here? Because I don't know how long I can stay in this place before my skin starts crawling! Ugh! Do you have roaches and shit like that? Because I'm allergic!"

"Damarr should be here soon," I said trying to keep my cool. I just kept reminding myself that I was doing this to get my cousin away from Cashay's fat ass.

"Well, he needs to hurry the hell up!" she enthused. Shit, I was with her on that. Damarr definitely needed to hurry the hell up!

At that moment, she started screaming and jumped on my kitchen counter. "What the hell is wrong with you?"

"Oh my God! You don't see that roach crawling on your wall!" she cried.

Looking over at the wall, sure enough, there was a huge cockroach crawling. I just grabbed my slipper off the floor and slapped the shit out of it... literally.

After I got a sheet of paper towel off the counter, I removed the dead roach off my shoe then tossed it in the trash. "You can get down off my counter now!" I said through clenched teeth.

"Eww! You got roaches!"

"Girl, get your ass off my damn counter!"

"I just told you that I'm allergic to roaches!"

"Did it bite you?" I asked with a smirk on my face.

"No! Thank God!"

"Then you have nothing to worry about. I killed it so I don't think it's coming back. Besides, Damarr will be here any minute now. If you wanna surprise him, you can wait in the bedroom."

"Oh God! Is it even safe in there?" she asked.

"Shit, it might be safer for you in there than out here because you are really pissing me off!"

Chandra looked at me with fright in her eyes as she slowly climbed off the counter. She followed me into the bedroom and started complaining immediately.

What is wrong with this bitch?!

"Oh my God! Do you ever clean?"

"Bitch shut up!"

"Stop calling me a bitch! You don't know me!"

"And you don't know me!" I warned.

KNOCK! KNOCK! KNOCK!

"That might be Damarr!"

"Thank God!" she hissed. "I am so ready to get out of this place! The fact that you don't see nothing wrong with how you live is beyond me girl! Like eww! Just gross!"

"Just stay your fucking ass in here for a few minutes so I can break the news to him that you're here. Just give me a few minutes then you can come out," I said.

"Oh God! I hope I can last a few minutes in this pigsty! Girl, you are nasty!" Chandra continued as she made a stank face.

"I ain't a killer bitch, but you pushing me! You are really pushing me!" I said as I held up my finger while shaking it at her before I exited the room.

If I had known that bitch was like this, I never would've invited her here. Now, I understood why Damarr wanted to get away from her ass. I wished I hadn't gotten involved because now all that I wanted to do was get away from her. I just hoped my cousin had the decency to hear me out before he jumped the gun and busted my chops.

Rushing to the door to open it, instead of Damarr standing there, it was kids selling some fucking cookies. Slamming the door back in their faces, I shook my head. I couldn't believe Chandra's reaction to my place. Bitch acted like she lived in Buckingham Palace or something.

Just for her acting all stuck up and shit, I left her ass right there in that room. That was just where she would stay until Damarr got here.

That's the only place that bitch is safe right now!

Chapter Fifteen

Cashay

If it wasn't Demisha being messy, it was this bitch from Damarr's past. Although she lived in Arkansas, she had been calling to Houston to stir up shit.

"Just as long as the bitch stays away from me!" I told Damarr after I finally got Katrice to give me some privacy.

Sure, she probably meant well by trying to hook me and Tay up, but her timing was off. Especially when I had already given up my goodies to Damarr! To me, that meant everything, and I prayed that he was feeling the same way.

Besides, Tay lived in Hawaii and would only be in town for a couple of weeks. Why even start something with him when he would be leaving anyway?

Erasing the entire idea from my head, I hung up with Damarr and went into the kitchen to make myself a plate. Katrice could cook her ass off and that food was smelling good!

"So, you tell ol' boy that you were going out with me today?" Tay asked the second I stepped back into the kitchen. He wasn't letting up for nothing.

"You are funny Tay!"

"I'm not trying to be Cashay. I'm trying to spend some time with you. If that ain't what you want, just say the word and I'll back up and give you your space."

"No, I didn't mean it like that Tay!" I insisted not wanting to hurt his feelings or come off the wrong way.

It wasn't like this guy was ugly and homeless or anything like that. Tay was quite the opposite. He was tall, had a light brown flawless skin complexion, a body to die for, a bomb ass career and was more intelligent than any other guy I had met. I mean, I wouldn't expect him to be any other way since he was in the military. He had to be in shape to be in the Army.

Maybe it was his intellect that intimidated me. Everything about him reeked prestigious and it wasn't nothing prestigious about fucking with me.

Shit, I was just a normal schoolteacher with an income that I could barely survive off of. I had a college degree from a community college and hadn't even been out of the state of Texas in my life!

Nah, Tay was making a bad decision by trying to push up on me. He was older and way out of my league!

"Stop acting like that Cashay! Just give me that chance. Spend the day with me and if you don't see yourself looking at me differently by the end of the night, I'll back off. I promise," Tay said getting all up in my face.

His boldness and wordplay were definitely doing a number on me. Katrice cheering on the sidelines didn't help out either. What was I going to do?!

"Fine. I'll spend the day with you. Just remember what you promised," I said.

"I got you," Tay said. "I'm gonna head to the hotel room so I can freshen up and change clothes..."

"What? No uniform?" Katrice asked.

"Nope. Civilian clothes today. Be back soon."

"I'll be ready when you get back," I said.

Tay rushed out the door happier than I had seen him in a long time. "Well, I'm glad you're going out with Tay. I know you're feeling Damarr, especially after last night, but it means a lot that you're spending some time with my cousin."

"I only agreed so he could see that there ain't nothing between us, so he can get over whatever it is he thinks he's feeling," I pointed out.

"I don't know Cashay. He seems real sure about how he feels. For whatever reason you said yes, I hope y'all have a great time."

"We'll see."

I wasn't sure what Tay was hoping for, but I wasn't about to fake anything just to make him happy. If I wasn't feeling it, I was definitely going to let him know it. I didn't want him or Katrice getting their hopes up about anything.

"So, are you going to tell Damarr about your date?" Katrice asked.

"It's not a date! It's just two childhood friends spending some time together," I corrected.

"So, are you going to tell Damarr or not?"

"I don't have to tell him anything. He doesn't keep tabs on me like that!" I said. "I'll just tell him that I have something that came up."

"So, y'all had plans for the evening?"

"Not really. When I left this morning, we just said we'd talk later."

"Well, good. That way he won't be expecting you," Katrice said.

"I just don't want him to think I'm blowing him off after what happened between us last night."

"He's a big boy. He'll be fine. Besides, from what I understand, he has plenty to worry about with his ex."

"Girl, stop! He ain't worried about that girl!"

"Or so he tells you," Katrice snickered.

"I'm gonna go get ready," I replied waving her off.

There was no time to be worrying myself with what Katrice was talking about when I was already nervous about spending time with Tay.

Considering the way that he said he felt about me, I didn't know what to expect.

With my day weighing heavy on my mind, I hopped in the shower and washed myself again. When I was done, I turned the water off, stepped out, dried off and began to get ready for my outing with Tay.

Not sure where we were going, I wanted to dress in something cute and comfortable. After digging through my closet, I chose to wear a pair of acid wash cropped boyfriend jeans. To match perfectly, I picked a red shirt with frills and ruffled sleeves. The neckline wasn't plunging but it definitely showed a little cleavage.

My hair was all over, so in order to get it somewhat tamed, I threw it up in a messy bun then applied a little makeup and slipped my feet into a pair of brown sandals. There was no denying, I looked good.

"Not bad for a big girl," I commented as I twirled in the mirror.

It was at that moment I heard the doorbell chime. An hour and a half had passed, so I headed to the front because I knew it was Tay returning. As soon as I stepped into the living room area, his eyes were on me like a hungry wolf.

"You look amazing!" he complimented, confirming what I already knew.

"Thank you," I replied with a smile.

"You two have fun, and don't do nothing I wouldn't do," Katrice clowned.

"We bout to do everything your lil boring ass wouldn't do!" Tay responded back, causing the three of us to break into laughter.

"You ready to go?" Tay asked me.

As I nodded my head affirmatively, he gently clinched my hand and led me out to his Jeep. Opening my door like the gentleman he was, I smiled and thanked him. Buckling up for safety, I watched as Tay climbed into the driver's seat and stared me down before keying the ignition.

"Where are we going?" I questioned.

"You'll see."

While he drove to Lord only knew where, we made conversation about how things had been going for us over the past decade or so since we last saw one another. When he pulled into the parking lot of Buffalo Bayou Park, my eyes widened.

"What are we doing here?"

"You'll see," he said with a smile.

After Tay quickly hopped out of the truck, he ran around and opened my door, helping me out. He held my hand and led me to the boat rentals.

"What's this?"

"We're going kayaking," Tay announced with a smile. "Have you ever been?"

"No! I've never been kayaking! Do you see how fat my ass is?" I gasped looking at him like he was crazy. "You tryna clown me thinking I can fit in that little ass boat?"

Even though he probably didn't mean to offend me, I was feeling some kind of way right now.

"You are not fat! You are fine, sexy and beautiful," he said as he looked into my eyes.

"You don't have to say nice things to me to make me feel good Tay. I look at myself every morning and every night."

"Then you must see the same gorgeous woman that I see. Sure, you have a little more meat on your bones, but I don't know one man who doesn't like a voluptuous female. I know that I do," he confessed proudly. "Now, let's try kayaking and if you don't like it, we'll come back with the boat and do something else."

"Okay."

"Okay, but if this fucking boat tips over Tay! So help me, I'm gonna swim to shore, wait for you and pop you a good one!" I promised as he helped me into the boat and then he got in the back.

"See, this ain't so bad, right?" he asked.

"We haven't even started paddling yet," I laughed nervously.

"Then let's get to it."

The two of us began to paddle the boat down the bayou. After about ten minutes, my nerves began to settle. As me and Tay talked, I realized what a good time I was actually having. I had never done anything like this before, and if it hadn't been for Tay, I probably wouldn't have ever even tried it out.

"Are you having fun?" he checked.

"Surprisingly, yes! I've never done anything like this before, but I'm really enjoying myself," I admitted.

For the next half hour, we rode in the boat having a grand old time. Then it was time to return it. As my high came down, Tay and I walked to his Jeep and he got a blanket from the back. Then we went to the food truck and ordered chili dogs, fries and drinks.

With our hands full, Tay found a very beautiful oak tree near the fountain. He spread the blanket out, placed the food down then we sat.

"Thanks for coming out with me," he spoke kindly while looking me in the eyes.

"Thanks for inviting me. I'm having a really good time," I replied with butterflies dancing inside.

"I'm glad. I know you were thinking that I was clowning about my interest in you, but I just want you to know that I'm serious. I'm really feeling you..."

"I know what you said Tay, but even if I gave you a chance, you're leaving for Hawaii in two weeks. What's gonna happen when you leave? I can't move to Hawaii, and I'm not sure I can do a long- distance relationship."

"We can figure that out once we decide where this is going."

"I don't know Tay..."

"So, you aren't feeling this?" he asked.

"Feeling what?" I inquired.

Without any warning, Tay leaned in towards me and gently pressed his lips against mine causing a spark that left my lady part throbbing. Tay's lips were so soft and tasted like chili. My greedy ass wanted to eat them up, but the thought of giving my goodies to Damarr last night had me abruptly pulling away.

"I'm sorry. Did I do something wrong?" Tay asked with a worried expression on his face.

"No, you didn't. It's me," I confessed.

"I like you Cashay. I know it might be a little weird since you think of me as a brother or something, but I'm not your brother nor your cousin. I'd like us to get to know each other as adults and if you're not comfortable with us being in a relationship, maybe we can just spend time together and keep in touch after I'm gone," he offered.

"We can do that. Keep in touch after you're gone, I mean," I clarified.

"Cool. At least you're not writing me off completely," Tay responded with a slightly disappointed expression.

"Well, I would have if we hadn't come out here today," I replied honestly with a smile.

"Well, I don't want this date to end. How about we go to the Aquarium or something? Then we can go out to dinner."

"Sure, why not?"

"I can't think of a reason..."

So, that was what we did. We went to the Aquarium and then out to dinner at Outback Steakhouse. By the end of the night, I was seeing Tay in a totally different light... just like he said.

It was odd how I was able to put Damarr out of my head so quickly. Was it a sign? Was this all a test?

Hell, I honestly didn't know, nor care at the time. Enjoyment was the only thing on my mind...

Chapter Sixteen

Damarr

"What the hell?!" I huffed in irritation after I couldn't reach Cashay for the past two hours.

This chick wasn't answering her phone and that made me feel some type of way after finally crossing the line with her. Truthfully, I thought it was something special, but obviously Cashay didn't. She hadn't hollered at me since she left the night before!

As I angrily paced the floor, I felt the vibration in my hand. Lifting my phone up without checking, I answered.

"Hello."

"Hey cuz, you busy?" Demisha asked.

"What do you need?"

"I need your help with a clog."

"Da fuck!"

"In my kitchen sink. I've tried plunging it, but it won't unclog," she huffed.

"Don't you live in an apartment? Why not just call the apartment manager?"

"Boy you know darn well we live in the hood! Ain't nobody coming out to check no pipes on the weekends over here!" she expressed. "Please cuz. I wouldn't ask if it wasn't important."

Taking in a deep breath, I closed my eyes and exhaled slowly. Questioning this shit in my head, I became frustrated even more.

'Why me?'

Biting the bullet, I went ahead and gave in only because I knew my cousin. She wouldn't stop bugging me until I agreed to come over and help her out.

"Fine! I'll be there in a couple of hours," I relented.

"That's perfect! Thanks cousin!"

We ended the call and I tried reaching out to Cashay again. The phone rang four times before going to voicemail. This time, I decided to leave a message since I hadn't left one any of the other times I called.

As I finished and set my cell down, I admitted to myself that I was kind of in my feelings since I still hadn't heard from her. Especially after she had expressed to me that it had been a while since she had allowed a man to make love to her. With that being said, I thought last night would have put the two of us in a much better place. I mean, first she ran out of there after four o'clock in the morning. What was the rush if she didn't have to work today?

It wasn't like she was going to get punished if she wasn't in bed by a certain time. She was a grown ass woman. So, not only did she run out at the crack of dawn this morning, but she didn't call me not one fucking time!

Immediately shifting my thoughts, I wondered what kind of game Cashay was playing because whatever it was, I didn't like it one bit. Picking my phone right back up, I left her a second message.

"Hey Cashay, I was just calling to check on you and see how you were doing. I also wanted to let you know that I had a great time last night. I hope you did too. Hit me up when you get the chance."

Pressing the red icon on my screen, I stood and went to get ready to head to Demisha's place. I hated going to the damn projects. Not that I was too good to go there, but because I had left those days behind me a long time ago. Every time I went to the projects, it brought back awful memories for me of when I was younger.

"I hope that this girl's clog ain't too severe, and I can hit it with the plunger a couple of times and be out." I thought aloud as I stopped by Walmart on my way and got a bottle of Draino. That way, once I unclogged the drain, I could pour the drain cleaner in it and that would prevent her from having anymore clogs for a while.

"Look at the shit right here! This is just the shit I was talking about!" I complained as I pulled into the parking lot about 20 minutes later to find it filled with unruly kids playing ball, jumping rope and riding bicycles.

There wasn't one fucking parent in sight. Demisha's kids were out there as well, but why would I expect anything different?

Shaking my head as I veered my car into an empty spot, I got out and walked to her apartment door and started knocking. After all that bugging me to come over in a hurry like it was a damn emergency, Demisha took forever to come and open it.

"Thank you so much for coming Damarr!" she said with a huge ass smile like she was up to something. With Demisha, you just never knew.

"Let me just unclog this damn drain so I can be on my way. I got way better things to do than spend my afternoon in your kitchen," I complained as I walked into the small kitchen.

Directing myself straight to the sink, I looked inside and didn't find any standing water. Now, I was confused.

To make sure that I wasn't tripping, I turned the water on, and sure enough, it flowed right down the drain. Glancing up with a confused expression, I found Demisha standing there with an amused look on her face.

"Oops!" she clowned.

"What the fuck yo! Why the hell you lie like that? Got me coming all the way over here for nothing! I had shit to do today man!" I fussed.

Hell, yeah, I was mad as fuck because she lived an hour away from my place. Coming all the way over here was a huge inconvenience yet she was standing there like it wasn't shit. The fucking nerve of her! Cousin or not, Demisha was about to get cussed out.

"Sorry cuz. I didn't mean to lie to you…"

"Then why did you?" I asked.

"Look, I don't want you to be mad at me, but I thought that you could use some help in your personal life."

"Fa real! What the fuck made you think that shit?" I snapped. "If you had anything to say to me Demisha, you could've said that shit over the phone or through a text! You got me way over here, all out of my fucking way, for some bullshit advice that you think you need to give me?!"

While I was in the midst of letting Demisha have it for playing childish games, I heard the door to the back bedroom open up. Assuming it was one of her kids, I ignored it until I saw Chandra making her way down the hallway.

Seriously! I could have slapped the shit out of Demisha right now! Even though Chandra was looking just as beautiful as ever, deep inside I knew that crazy side of her wasn't too far.

"My God! I've had just about all I can take in that filthy ass room!" Chandra said dramatically as she fanned herself. She rushed over to me and threw her arms around me. "Oh, thank God you're here!"

"What the fuck Demisha?! What is she doing over here?" I asked angrily.

"Look cuz, normally I'd stay out of your business..."

"You should've kept that momentum going!" I smirked. "I mean, what possessed you to get involved with my fucking business!"

"Don't be mad at her baby. I asked your cousin to get you over here. I would've much rather go to your place, but I didn't have the address, and Demisha wouldn't give it to me without your permission." Demisha stood there with a smug look on her face like she wanted a prize for not divulging my information. "Anyway, I kind of twisted her arm to get you here because we really need to talk," Chandra continued.

"You must be out of your damn mind! I told you already that we have nothing to talk about Chandra! You just wasted your time coming here!"

"I don't think so. Like I told you we need to have a conversation!"

"Ain't nothing to talk about," I adamantly responded.

"Uh, not to get in your business cuz..."

"It's a little too late for that shit, don't you think Demisha?!" I asked as I rolled my eyes at her.

"I know, but this girl said she's pregnant and the baby is yours. So, I'd say y'all have a lot to talk about," Demisha intervened.

"You don't even know the full story behind this shit Demisha! That's why you should've stayed out of it! So, how many times does this make that you told me you were pregnant Chandra? What, seven, eight? And still never had one baby! Not one!" I clowned as I held up my finger.

"What?!" Demisha asked with a smirk on her face. "So, you're not pregnant?" She directed her question and attention to Chandra.

"Of course, I'm pregnant!" Chandra said, but something told me that silly grin on her face meant she was lying once again.

"Look, I'm outta here! I ain't got time for these bullshit games you keep trying to play!" I said as I tried to make my way towards the exit. "You really should've kept your ass in Little Rock!"

Chandra jumped out in front of me, threw her arms around me, and started crying like her life depended on it. "Please don't leave! Don't leave me here baby! Just being in this apartment has my skin itching!" she said as she shuddered while rubbing her arms.

"Excuse me bitch!" Demisha chimed in angrily. She hated when people talked about where she lived because it was all she could afford. It didn't matter who it was, she would flip out.

"I'm not a bitch!" Chandra cried. "Please take me away from this ratchet hell hole of an apartment! I ain't never been subjected to no type of living like this! Look at her floors! They're so filthy I bet she ain't mopped since Moses parted the Red Sea!"

"If you don't quit with the insults, I'm about to split your fuckin' wig in half just like Moses did the Red Sea! I keep telling you that you don't know me! Keep playing with me!" Demisha warned.

Chandra acted like she never heard anything Demisha said as she continued. "And her bedroom looks like a tornado blew threw it! Don't even get me started on the stench coming from the bathroom! Enough to make me puke out everything I ate this morning!"

"Okay now, bitch! Ain't gon' be too much more of that shit talking about my place! I was nice enough to try and help you get back with my cousin, but I'm warning you!" my cousin responded angrily. "You got one mo fuckin' time!"

"See, she's even threatening me baby! You can't just leave me here after I came all this way for you!" Chandra cried.

"I didn't ask you to come all the way over here!" I said as I tried to get her off me. "I can't tell you where to go, but I can tell you that you ain't coming with me!"

"So, even though I'm having your baby, you're still gonna leave me high and dry!"

While all the chaos was going on, the front door opened up, quieting us all. As we stared towards the front, up pops some random nigga. I didn't know if he was Demisha's boyfriend or one of her baby daddies. The only thing I was certain of was he was one of her worthless ass niggas!

"What the fuck is going on here?" the dude asked as he looked at the three of us.

"Terrance? What you doing just walking in my apartment like that?" Demisha questioned boldly stepping forward. "Where the hell they do that at?"

"Woman don't be asking me no fucking question about what I'm doing here! You know why the fuck I'm here! The question is what the fuck is they doing here?" the dude asked with a scowl on his face.

"Look Terrance! You don't pay rent and I ain't neva gave you a fucking key, so I don't know what made you think it was okay for you to just let yourself in!" Demisha yelled as Chandra held onto me tightly.

"I ain't need no damn key! You left your door unlocked fool!" Terrance said with a laugh.

"Damn Damarr! You left the fucking door unlocked?!" Demisha asked as she glared at me before rolling her eyes.

"Shit, I didn't know muthafuckas would be bold enough to be running in and outta here like this!" I told Demisha as she went right back in on the Terrance dude.

That was my cue to get to stepping right out the door. Thinking that I was escaping Chandra as well, I ran and hopped in my car. Just as I keyed the ignition, here she come flying out the apartment. Jumping into my passenger seat uninvited, Chandra told me that I was not leaving her here for another minute.

"I didn't tell you to come over here in the first place! Matter of fact, why you bring yo ass down here Chandra?! I told you on the phone it was over, and I was done!" I flipped. "How the fuck you get here anyway?!"

"I drove, but I parked down the street so you wouldn't see my car. I wanted to surprise you!" she cheered.

"Bitch! You went to Suga Mama's and fucked up both my rides! That was all the fucking surprise I needed from yo ass! And now, you wanna bring yo ass down here like we cool and shit!"

Seriously ready to put her out my shit, I pulled over once we got to the front of the complex. "Get the fuck out!"

"Are you really gonna just put me out in the middle of nowhere when I'm carrying your baby?"

"Where's the fucking proof Chandra?! You done hollered that shit so many fucking times I don't believe you!" I yelled until she shut me up with a damn pregnancy paper stamped with her doctor's seal.

Sure, it could've been fake or forgery, but it appeared real enough to have a nigga sweating bullets. Not knowing how far along she was, I took the time to read the entire document.

"It's not too late for you to get rid of it! I'm gonna take you to the clinic so we can see what's really going on!" I insisted until I saw a flashy ride pull up in Demisha's parking lot.

It seemed way out of place seeing that I was sitting in the projects. Looking closer as it parked and a female got out, I saw that it was Lucca in the driver's seat.

Confirmed once he stepped out and I got a better look at him, I watched as he walked the chick to the door and followed her inside. The whole time, Chandra was watching me!

"Who the fuck is that bitch?!"

"Shut the hell up with all that noise! I don't even know who the girl is! I just know the dude!"

"If I didn't know any better, I would've thought that nigga was Legend! The one who got famous online with his guitar!"

"Yea, that was him!" I acknowledged as I sat debating on whether I should share the info or not.

While Chandra sat there going on and on about how talented that nigga Legend was, I debated on telling Cashay once I did get to talk to her. Because as of right then, I still hadn't heard from her!

Looking over at Chandra, I realized it didn't even pay for me to wonder about Cashay. My current situation would have me looking like a damn fool. I had to find a way to get rid of Chandra's ass!

I was still wondering what's up with Cashay not calling me though. That's some straight bullshit!

Chapter Seventeen

Lucca aka Legend

When I saw one of my old classmates, Lauren, at the gas station begging for money, I couldn't help but reach out. Giving her dough wasn't enough for her though. She wanted a ride home as well.

Taking the chance, I zipped her around the corner to the projects and prayed that I didn't get spotted by anyone. If I didn't have to piss so badly, I would've dropped her off and kept it pushing.

I didn't think I'd get caught going inside her dimly lit apartment, so I headed inside behind her. The place reeked of stale smoke and old food. Ugh! The shit made me sick to my stomach.

There was no evidence of kids there, so I didn't ask about it. I just took my ass straight to the bathroom, pissed and washed my hands. When I came out, the chick was butt ass naked with her phone in her hand.

"Yoooooo! What the fuck?!" I gasped trying to make it to the door as fast as I could.

"Let's just get a few good flicks together Lucca! You know how much money I could get for these?!" she screamed tackling me as she snapped picture after picture.

Panicking that shit would get worst, I tried for the door again. Only when I finally got it opened, Lauren was right on me again! By now, we done got a whole crowd gathering and I couldn't be caught like that.

Covering my face with my hoodie, I fiercely shook all those people loose and took off to the car. Locking my doors, I shot out of that lot mad at myself for trying to do a good deed.

Damn! I can't trust no fucking body!

Hopping on my cell, I dialed up my manager and told him what happened so that he could try to get a jumpstart on hushing that shit up before it went viral. So much for that idea because as soon as I got off the line with him, Katrice was calling me.

Feeling her out, I let her speak first. The way she was acting nonchalant, I figured that she hadn't gotten wind of the shit yet.

Yea, a nigga wasn't so lucky! Two or three minutes into the conversation, she started yelling.

"No fucking way!" Katrice hollered.

"What?! What is it?!" I pressed hoping that it wasn't what I thought it was.

"Lucca! How could you?!" she whined. "See! That's just why I didn't want to fuck with you in the first place! Cuz of shit like this!"

"I'm telling you Katrice! It wasn't nothing like that shit!" I tried to explain, but it wasn't getting me anywhere.

After she hung up on me and I watched the video on Facebook once I was tagged a dozen times, I understood why Katrice was so angry. From the looks of the recording, it seemed all the way foul!

"Whatever Lucca! You just do you and keep me as a friend! There's no way that I'm gonna be competing with your nasty ass groupies! When you get all that wild shit out of you, then call me!"

Katrice really hung up on me! Had my head so fucked up that I had to pull over and park the car to call her back.

"What the hell! Did she block me?!" I hissed in disbelief! That shit hadn't happened to me since high school.

Since becoming famous, I hadn't really had problems keeping a female. Katrice, she was definitely different and worth chasing after. At least in my eyes she was!

Making a hasty decision, I dipped down the block and jumped on the highway to go over to Katrice's to see if I could get her to talk to me.

"Damn, we just barely started dating and I done fucked up already!" I sighed as my cell continued to ring nonstop.

Not picking up until I saw my manager's name, I expected to hear some good news. "What's up?"

"I got the main link deleted, but the damage is already done. Let me think of a way to spin this mess before you go online trying to explain yourself," he suggested. "Don't want you to do more harm than good."

Agreeing wholeheartedly, I hung up with some type of hope that Katrice would forgive me for that stupid shit. "It wasn't nothing though!"

Once I got to Katrice's house, I saw a couple of different vehicles parked in the driveway. One was hers and the other I didn't recognize.

Parking out front, I dialed her up again only to find out that I was really blocked. That shit was messed up because we needed to talk. This was all just a simple misunderstanding that could be explained if she gave me the chance.

Only debating about it for another minute or two, I finally got my ass out the car and went up to knock on the door. Instead of Katrice answering it, she chose to open the window and speak with me like that.

"Now why would you just show up over here when I told you how I felt Lucca?"

"You just gonna talk to me like this? You not gonna let me in?"

"No, I'm not!"

"Come on now Katrice! That video was foul, but I can promise you that it's not at all what you think."

"How the hell you know what I'm thinking?" she asked angrily.

"Because I know. But trust me, it ain't like what you obviously think it is! If you just let me in, I'll prove it to you," I reasoned knowing that I couldn't prove a thing. All I had was my word and if she let me in, I was sure that I could convince her that I did nothing wrong. "You know I leave tomorrow for a week baby! You gonna let me leave with us arguing like this over nothing?"

"You were over some chick's house when she was butt ass naked Lucca! I saw that shit with my own eyes! It's not like it's some 'he said, she said' shit! I saw it!" Katrice fussed like her feelings were crushed.

Seeing her like that broke my heart. The last thing that I wanted to do was hurt her. She meant way too much to me and right now I needed to show her. But how?

"Come on Katrice," I pleaded but all I got was the middle finger and the window slammed in my face.

Part of me wanted to give up while the other part wanted to kick in the door and make Katrice listen to me. Both possibilities made me a loser and that wasn't an option.

"Are you fucking kidding me?!" I yelled out into the darkness as I started to get dampened by the raindrops.

For some dumb ass reason, all I could picture was that scene from Tiffany Haddish's movie where her sister sung to get her man back out in the rain. Thinking that it could actually work, I ran and jumped into the car and parked it as close as I could to the front door.

Leaving my car doors wide open, I put my new song on and blasted it as loud as possible. As I listened to my voice project through the speakers, I overpowered it and poured my heart out.

Katrice may not have come out right away, but after her neighbors started to show up to watch, she couldn't help herself. "Lucca!"

"I'm so sorry baby!" I told her as she ran towards my open arms.

While I was thinking it was about to be a special moment, Katrice bypassed me, rolled my windows up, cut the music off, killed the engine and shut my doors. When she finished, she popped me a good one and pulled me inside.

With all the cell cameras on us, I knew I would be in the media again. Twice in one night!

Chapter Eighteen

Katrice

No matter how hard I tried to be mad at Lucca, I couldn't. He was such a sweet person I couldn't help but fall for him. That was why my feelings were getting hurt every time that he had some type of incident with one of his fans.

The shit was so overwhelming that it made me hesitate to go forward with our relationship. I mean, why? What for? If we got married or anything like that, the same shit would be happening. As long as Lucca was famous, I couldn't see us being together in peace. That shit broke my heart too because I really had strong feelings for him!

Just as I opened my mouth to speak to him about how I was feeling, here comes Tay and Cashay through the front door. With all the giggling and shit they were doing I knew they must've been lit.

"Who drove?" I asked.

"I did and I'm straight cousin!" Tay laughed and he looked at Lucca. "Legend?"

"Hey, what's up Tay?" he greeted with a handshake and some dap.

While the two men started a whole conversation to catch up, I drew Cashay in the other room to see how their date went. Before she could spill the beans, her cell went off.

Cashay ignored it at least three times before I asked her what was going on. Hell, I should've already known.

"Damarr girl!" she whispered. "He's been calling and texting me since I left with Tay!"

"You ain't answered him?"

"Honestly Katrice, I was having such a good time that I left my cell in the car after he wouldn't let up. I had the time of my life girl! Thank you for convincing me to go!"

"What?!" I shouted happily. I couldn't believe it. It was like music to my ears!

Sure, I liked Cashay with Damarr, but he was street and had too much baggage! Now my cousin Tay, he was perfect for her! At least in our eyes he was.

"Yes! We had so much fun Katrice! We did things I ain't never done before!" she said making me give her a dirty look.

"Like what?!"

"Not like that girl!" she hissed and cut her eyes. "I just slept with Damarr last night! I'm not a bed hopping ho!"

"I didn't say that you were boo! I just wanna know what you plan to do?" I asked curiously.

"I plan on exploring my options! I mean, look at the drama that Damarr is going through! This bitch Chandra is all the way back in Arkansas stirring up some shit! Just imagine if she showed up down here with all that shit!" Cashay complained and I knew how she felt.

There wasn't no man worth fighting with other bitches over. There were too many in this world to be tripping over one!

"Enough about me Katrice! When we walked in, I felt the tension!" Cashay questioned forcing me to pull my cell out and show her the video.

As her mouth dropped, she pushed the phone away and hugged me. "I'm so sorry sis! That shit has to be a lot to take. I really don't think that there's too much to it, but I do question why he was over there in the first place. Maybe he has a reasonable explanation. Have you even given him a chance?"

"No! And why you worrying about me, what are you gonna tell Damarr about you not answering your phone all damn day? Huh Cashay?" I pressed.

"Shit, I don't know and I'm not gonna worry about that right now. I'm about to go in the other room and play some dominoes. You and Lucca down?"

"You are crazy Cashay! You know that girl?"

"Yes, I am and yes I do! Now let's go in there with the fellas before they come looking for us!" she teased.

We headed to the front room where we played dominoes until well into the night. Even though I was still feeling some kind of way about Lucca and the groupie from earlier, I decided to let it go. He had his attention focused all on me and after he explained everything to me, I believed him. After he promised that he would never let himself be in a position like that again, I promised I wouldn't bring it up again. Once we got that shit straight, we began drinking.

By the time midnight rolled around, we were all good and lit. Cracking up, I watched Tay and Cashay as they clowned and poked fun at each other throughout the night. I was happy that she gave my cousin a chance. I wasn't sure where their relationship would go once that he left for Hawaii, but I hoped that she would continue to date him. Hell, I could definitely use a trip to Hawaii.

Checking the time again, I saw that it was almost 2am. It was getting late, and I was getting antsy so and Lucca went to my room, leaving Cashay and Tay snuggling on the sofa watching a movie.

Just like I anticipated too! When I woke up the next morning, they were right where we left them. Wrapped in each other's arms but still fully clothed. Immediately smiling, I glanced down at the two of them.

"Shit!" I whispered as Cashay's phone started vibrating.

Assuming that I already knew who it was, I walked over to the coffee table where her phone was to try and silence it before they woke up. Taking a peek at the screen before doing so, I saw that it was Damarr, so I decided to answer.

Hurrying to the back patio for privacy, I closed myself out and connected the call.

"Hello," I answered in a hushed tone.

"Hello. May I speak to Cashay?"

"She's asleep. I can tell her that you called," I offered.

"Please do. I've been trying to reach her since yesterday, but she hasn't been picking up."

"Oh, well, I don't know nothing about that. But I will let her know that you called."

"Thanks."

"No problem."

To ensure that Damarr didn't disturb my bff, I silenced Cashay's phone as soon as I hung up on him. It wasn't that I was trying to keep them apart, I just didn't think it was a good time for them to speak seeing that Tay was still there.

When Cashay woke up, I would let her know why I turned it off. Until then, I wasn't about to worry myself with it. Not with my stomach growling.

Initially, I was going to cook breakfast, but since there were four of us instead of two, I decided to order with Door Dash. Settling on Krush Bistro & Bar, I ordered steak and eggs for Tay and Lucca and chicken and waffles for me and Cashay. After adding four large cups of orange juice, I paid online.

While waiting on the food, I went to the bathroom to brush my teeth and wash my face before relieving myself. When I exited the bathroom, Lucca was stirring in the bed. I watched as he felt for me on my side of the bed, and when he didn't feel my body, he looked up and saw me standing there.

"Good morning beautiful," he greeted with a smile.

"Good morning to you."

"What are you doing all the way over there?" he flirted.

"I just ordered breakfast for all of us."

"Okay. What did you order?"

"Steak and eggs for you and Tay. I figured the two of you needed a hearty meal."

"Thanks babe," he said with a smile.

"You're welcome."

"Do you have to go and pick it up?"

"No. They're coming to deliver it," I told him with a curious smile.

"So, why don't you come lay back down with me until they get here?" he suggested.

"Okay, but don't try nothing."

"You saying that cuz you want me to try something," he flirted as he moved over for me. "You ain't fooling nobody."

As I slid in bed, I pressed my back against his front. "I ain't doing nothing to fool nobody," I giggled.

"Uh huh. Okay." As he held me from behind, I felt him inhale deeply. I wondered what was on his mind.

"What's wrong?"

"Nothing."

"Don't tell me nothing when it sounds like you have the weight of the world on your shoulders."

"It's not that. It's just that I feel bad about what happened yesterday. Thank God you believe me but think of all the fans who probably think I was fucking with that girl. When in actuality, all I was trying to do was help her out," he said.

"We don't have to keep talking about this Lucca. I wouldn't have said that I believed you if I didn't."

"I know. I'm glad you gave me a chance to explain because I don't know what I would've done if you had told me to kick rocks or something."

"I did tell you that," I reminded him.

"Yea, but you ain't saying that now," he said as he kissed my neck and rubbed his dick against my ass.

A slight moan escaped my lips as he slipped a hand inside my shorts and panties. I was about to give it to him until the doorbell rang.

"Saved by the bell." I giggled.

"Aw man," Lucca groaned as I dipped out of the bed.

Running to the door to get the food, I tipped the driver and took everything into the kitchen while loudly calling out 'breakfast'. It was enough to gain everyone's attention and they were all joining me at the dining room table 10 minutes later to sit down and eat. Right away, I could tell that today was going to be a good day.

At least I hoped that was the case...

Chapter Nineteen

Demisha

As if the drama between Damar and that bitch Chandra wasn't enough! Then here came Terrance busting up in my place looking for some food and sex. If it wasn't for my best friend Penny bringing the kids right after Damarr and Chandra left, he would've practically raped me!

Rushing me to get them put to bed, I came back into the bedroom about thirty minutes later to him butt naked on my bed stroking his shit! Oh, boy! Terrance was ready and by the look on his face, he wasn't about to take 'no' for an answer!

Shit, he had a lot of fucking nerves showing up like this after I hadn't seen or heard from him since the last time that we had sex, and that was three weeks ago. I hated when he did that because it made me feel used every single time.

So, why do I keep letting him in my bed? Because the sex is amazing!

No matter how good it felt, it was never satisfying afterwards, and I didn't wanna feel that way. I didn't want him to just come by when he was hungry or horny. I wanted someone who would want me for me. Someone who was proud to have me on his arm. Someone who didn't mind taking me out and showing me off to the world.

That was not Terrance, and I knew it. But I didn't have anyone else in my life at the moment, so Terrance was gonna have to do. Soon as Mr. Right came along, it was out the door for him and there was no turning back. There was no way that I deserved to settle for what Terrance was offering. Some meaningless sex and a once-a-month visit was definitely not enough for me! I needed a man 24/7 not part time!

"Ugh, why he gotta do me like that?!" I complained as woke up and found him gone after I had fed him and sexed him down good. He didn't even stay until the next morning.

The empty side of the bed was a reminder of how dirty Terrance was. Feeling frustrated, I went to the bathroom and took care of my personal hygiene before heading to the kitchen to make breakfast for the kids who I already heard up making noise.

Jamal, and Amari came out of their rooms soon as they smelled the bacon frying. Jordan exited a couple of minutes later.

"Amari go get your sister," I told my daughter.

"Okay mommy."

Strutting her little self into the bedroom she shared with Bree, Amari returned with her younger sister seconds later. As they all climbed up to the table and waited patiently for their food, I admired how well-mannered and well behaved my kids were.

Of course, sometimes they had moments when they were a little rambunctious and out of control, but what kid didn't have moments like that? That didn't make them bad kids.

Thinking about how good of a parent I was, I patted myself on the back as I sat down to eat with my children. The moment that happened, they started questioning me about going to Ma'Dear's house for lunch.

"We're gonna go to Ma'Dear's house at two. They're having a late lunch today," I said.

"Don't you have to help cook mommy?" Amari asked.

"Not today baby. I used some of my food stamps and bought some stuff for them to cook, so

I'm gonna let the old ladies do it this time," I said as we all giggled.

"You better not let Ma'Dear hear you say that!" Jamal warned.

"I won't."

I loved my kids with all my heart. No matter what people said about me or how we lived, they could never say that I was a bad mom. Everything I did was for my children and they knew that they were loved.

Truthfully, I never meant to have four kids, but I never regretted having any of them. Jamal was totally unplanned, but it didn't matter because I wanted to be a mom. It didn't even matter whether or not things worked out with me and his dad. I just wanted to have someone who would love me unconditionally since no one else seemed to.

Then when I got pregnant the second time, I really wanted a little girl. When I found out that I was having another son, I cried for a whole week. Then I embraced the fact that I was having another little boy. I picked Jordan's name out as soon as I found out about him.

The third time I got pregnant, it didn't matter what I had. As long as the baby was healthy. I didn't find out about the baby until I was almost five months because I had gained weight during my first two pregnancies, so I just thought I was fat. Sure, I felt the movements in my belly, but I thought that was gas.

Finding out that I was having a little girl was the best thing in the world. Of course, I had to get a bigger place. I couldn't have three kids living in a two bedroom. So, my Section 8 gave me a voucher for a three bedroom.

After having three kids, I really thought that I was done, but then I got pregnant again. When I first found out, I didn't know how I felt when I heard the doctor confirm the news. But I made sure that I signed the papers to tie my tubes as soon as I found out. There was no way I was going to be a single mother with five children. I could have four, but definitely no more!

"Can we be excused now?" Jamal asked with a mouth full of food.

"What's the hurry?" I asked.

"We were watching the new Sonic movie mama!" Jordan announced.

Soon as I nodded my head affirmatively, the little crumb snatchers ran right on out of here. The only one who stayed behind was Amari. She always helped me rinse the dishes and put them into the dishwasher.

"My little helper!" I grinned as we finished up. "Thanks baby girl!"

"Always mama!" She smiled and ran off to the back.

As I was about to exit the kitchen, I listened as my cell rang in the distance. Assuming that it was in my bedroom, I rushed back there to see who was calling me.

"What does he want?" I questioned myself as I saw that I had three missed calls from Terrance.

Not knowing what the hell could be so important, I started to dial him back. Only I couldn't complete my call because before I could hit send, Penny was chiming in on the other line.

"What's up BFF?" she greeted. "You know today they're having that sidewalk sale at the mall. I still got that dough we saved up for it!"

"Oh, hell yeah!" I cheered. "We gotta go after I take the kids to my grandmother's house to eat. I'll take them around one and drop them. My auntie already agreed to watch them!"

"Cool!" Penny said excitedly. "I'll be over there early so I can go with you to drop the kids off. I promised Amari that I was gonna redo her two French braids anyhow."

"Thanks BFF. It's so cute how you did the girls' hair! I don't know what I would do without your help sometimes Penny! You are truly a godsend!"

"Girl please! That's what friends are for! You betta get me while you can because once I find me a good man, I plan on having some kids of my own! Until then, I'm here to watch them whenever I can boo!" Penny assured.

"Thanks so much!" I spoke just as my line clicked again. "What does this nigga want?! He done called me ten times this morning!"

"Who?"

"Terrance!"

"He left already?!" Penny gasped.

"You know that nigga don't ever spend the night! That's how I know he got another bitch! It's okay though because we always practice safe sex!"

"Why? You can't get pregnant again!" Penny clowned.

"Yea, but I can catch something that penicillin can't cure! That's what I'm not tryna do! I gotta be here to raise my kids because none of their daddies are gonna step up and be there for them!"

"True that sis!" Penny agreed as my line rang again.

This time, I told her to hold on because it wouldn't take long. Answering the phone, I heard Terrance, but his voice was so distorted that I couldn't make out what he was saying.

"What?!" I repeated for the third time.

"These niggas just jumped me!" he whispered.

"Where are you?"

"I'm down by the park!"

"Don't you got your gun!" I questioned knowing that Terrance never left home without some type of weapon. The way these young folks moved in the streets they were never safe.

"That's why I'm calling you! I think I left it over there!" he said.

"Over where? Over here?" I asked in a panicky tone.

Running back to my room to search for the firearm, I couldn't find it anywhere. It was when I walked out into the hallway that I discovered just where it was!

BOOM!

The sound from a gun discharging rang throughout my apartment and caused my body to freeze. It was like I weighed a ton, and nothing could make me move.

"Demisha! Demisha!" I heard Terrance screaming from the phone.

Snapping out of it, I could hear my kids screaming and hollering. The sounds pierced my heart, and I was terrified to see what had happened.

"Demisha! Demisha!" Terrance continued to yell.

Not wanting to deal with him at the moment, I hung up only for it to bring me back on the line with Penny. She was so busy singing that she didn't hear me until I started screaming at the sight of Jordan who came out into the hallway holding the smoking gun.

"I'm sorry mama! I'm so sorry!" my baby boy cried.

"What happened?!" I screamed as tears streamed from my eyes.

"I didn't know it was real mama!" he cried. "I'm sorry! I didn't mean to shoot Jamal!"

"What the hell did he just say?!" Penny shouted. "Did he say he shot Jamal?!"

There was no way that I could deal with what was going on. It was all too much! Especially when Amari came out crying with blood all over her.

"I tried to wake Jamal up mama! He won't open his eyes!" she whined.

The sight of it all took me right on out. I didn't wake up until Penny was standing over me and the medics were rushing inside.

The only question that I could force out of my mouth was, "Is he dead Penny? Is my baby dead?!"

The tears streaming from her eyes made me think the worst. Now, all I wanted to do was die!

Chapter Twenty

Damarr

The next day, Chandra was still over at my house. The first night, it wasn't a big deal because we both fell asleep in the living room as soon as we got there.

Dipping off to my room in the middle of the night, I left Chandra on the sofa. Odd shit was that she was right beside me when I woke up the next morning.

"What's up with you?" I asked waking her up.

"I'm just so tired! They said having a baby would be rough on my body, but damn! This baby shit is really getting to me!"

"Shit, I need to know if you are really pregnant Chandra! We've been through this shit too many times for me to just take your word for it."

"After I done showed you the paperwork from the clinic and my doctor?" she whined. "What you need for me to do? Pee on a stick?"

"No, we're going to the clinic here!" I told her as I started getting dressed.

"All my clothes are in my car and its over at your cousin's place!" she informed me.

Picking up my cell ready to reach out to my cousin, I saw that my phone had been powered off. Thinking that it had died, I plugged it in and waited for it to charge.

"Let me see you phone right quick," I said to Chandra who freely gave it up like she didn't have shit to hide.

Taking it from her, I did an online search for a nearby clinic. Once I found one, I made an appointment for that afternoon.

"You want me to take you to get your car? You know they tow unauthorized vehicles from there if they're parked overnight and don't have a sticker?"

"Why the hell didn't you tell me that shit last night Damarr?!"

"I forgot!" I snapped back. "Calm yo ass down and let me give you some shorts and a t-shirt until we can get back over there."

"Just take me to the mall down the street. I'll get something there and we can go to the clinic right after."

Not wanting to be seen with her in public, I went ahead and let her take my ride. With her momentarily out of the way, I could make some phone calls in privacy.

Soon as I finally got her out of the door, I got my cell off the charger to see that it was fully charged. That meant that it wasn't dead in the first place! Yea, I knew Chandra shut my shit off on purpose.

That shit burned me up, but what could I do? The damage was already done!

Checking my call log to see if Cashay had reached out to me, I saw that I had no missed calls from her. Only calls that I had missed were from Demisha, my auntie, my uncle and some unknown number.

Assuming that all they wanted was to bug me about coming to lunch over at Ma'Dear's house, I ignored all the missed calls and focused on reaching out to Cashay.

This time, I only called twice and both times it went directly to the voicemail. That meant her phone was either dead or she had me blocked, which I didn't think she would do.

"Why am I being ignored though?!" I wondered out loud. "Was the sex that fucking bad?"

Ever since Cashay left after we finally got busy in the bedroom she was nowhere to be found. It was like she was trying to avoid me on purpose.

Never being the one to chase after a female, I pushed that shit to the side and ran through the shower before Chandra got back. I didn't need to be naked around her! No telling how she would react, and I wasn't trying to take it there with her.

Shit, I was still mad about her fucking my cars up back in Arkansas! Chandra was damn lucky that I had good insurance on them both!

With my patience running short, I listened as my cell rang with Demisha's number popping up. After the way she encouraged Chandra to bring her ass down to Houston, then set me up the way that she did, I didn't have shit to say to her ass! Cousin or not, she had crossed the fucking line!

Besides, I had some business to handle. I needed to know if Chandra was pregnant with my child or not.

"Please don't let this chick be pregnant!" I chanted as I tied my new ice white Air Force Ones up.

Just as I stood up, I heard the keys in the door. Yea, Chandra took it upon herself to use my keys to enter up in my shit without knocking. Made me think she may have another one made while she was gone.

Checking the time, I saw that Chandra had been gone well over an hour. That gave her plenty of time to be sneaky.

"You got all those bags! You shopped that fast?"

"Well, I knew what I wanted, so I chose a store that would have it all. I only had to go to one!" she explained as she waltzed off to the bathroom.

Chandra's presence was rubbing me the wrong way. When I left her in Arkansas, I never expected to see her again in life! I was just getting over her ass and then here she comes, popping up once again talking about she was pregnant!

Pacing the floor with worry, I began to think of a way to talk this girl out of having the baby if the test turned out positive. Sure, I cared about Chandra, but after sleeping with Cashay, I felt a stronger connection with her that I couldn't shake.

If I had to choose today, my choice would definitely be Cashay! Hands down! It didn't matter if Chandra was carrying my child or not because I couldn't see myself leaving Cashay alone.

"But she would leave me the fuck alone if this bitch is pregnant!" I whispered to myself. "Please don't let her be pregnant!"

Just as I finished up my little prayer, Chandra walked out of the bathroom looking and smelling like a million bucks. Wearing designer shit from head to toe was so country to me.

"I'm ready!" she told me as she grabbed my keys off the table like she was driving.

Snatching them right up out of her grip, I led the way out to the car and shot this broad right on over to the clinic down the street. When we got there, she was full of smiles and walked with confidence. That made me feel like she had no worries in the world.

Yea, she was pregnant, and it was confirmed right when she came out from the back grinning widely. Man, I could've just broken down in tears right there in the waiting room.

Being the man that I was, I sucked it up and we walked out to the car. Once inside, I began questioning Chandra about how far along she was.

"It doesn't matter what I say or what test I take Damarr, you just don't wanna believe that I'm actually having your baby for real this time!" Chandra huffed heavily like her feelings were hurt.

Fuck her damn feelings! I was the one who needed to be crying! I didn't want to be in a relationship with her and I certainly wasn't ready to raise no kids with her or no one else for that matter! I was still young and had plenty to do before that time came!

"No matter how hard you try Damarr, you're not gonna be able to wish this baby out of me! It's reality boo! We're gonna be parents! Do you believe that shit?"

"Hell nah!" I hissed and headed over to get her car. There was no way that I was about to have to chauffer her every time that she wanted to go somewhere.

"What the hell?!" Chandra screamed as we arrived near the projects 20 minutes later. "Where the fuck is my damn car?!"

"I told you that they tow cars after they've been sitting here for 24 hours!"

"You just told me that shit this morning!" she fussed. "Now what the hell am I gonna do?"

"I'll take you get your shit later."

I backed out of the parking spot and was leaving the lot when we noticed that they had the whole parking lot taped off. Part of it was ripped and there were no signs of emergency vehicles, so I assumed that whatever happened must've already been over.

"I wonder what the hell went on over there!" Chandra pondered.

"Probably another shooting up in there! Shit happens all the time. When I came over the first time, they were just taking some of that tape down," I explained.

"Well, what about my car? Where did they tow it?" she asked again when I had just told her ass.

"There's a sign right there. Take down the number and we can call and get it later." I said.

"That's fine with me!" Chandra replied happily.

At least one of us were happy because as each second passed and she was with me, I became more irritated with her presence. It was like her mouth was running nonstop and all she wanted to talk about was that fucking baby!

Well, until I found out that it was mine for sure, I wasn't about to dive into this commitment heart first! No buddy! This time, I would use my head and find out just what the hell was going on because best believe I wasn't about to let her pull one over on me! Not this time!

"What you wanna do now?" Chandra chanted bringing me out of my mental rant. "I'm hungry."

Swinging by a drive-thru pissed her off, but like I said, I wasn't about to be seen in public with her. Not when I had my heart set on being with Cashay.

Honestly, she was all I could think about since finding out that Chandra was pregnant. Now, how was I going to explain this shit?!

Chapter Twenty-One

Cashay

I hadn't spoken to Damarr in two days, and it was starting to bug me. If Tay hadn't been keeping me so busy, I would've reached out to him just to let him know that I wasn't acting funny or anything.

"Good morning!" Katrice greeted as I walked into the kitchen while she was pouring a cup of fresh brew. "You want one?"

"Sure, thanks sis!" I replied and popped two slices of bread in the toaster.

As Katrice and I sat there chatting, she filled me in on how well it was going with Lucca. Happy for her, I congratulated her on her newfound relationship.

"It's not all it's cracked up to be, but I really do like Lucca!" she admitted.

After sharing a few stories and finishing up our coffee, I went back in my room to check my phone. As usual, it was dead.

Bored out of my mind, I wound up falling asleep while waiting for it to fully charge. Now in a deep slumber, I began dreaming wildly about Tay. It was so strange because when I woke up a couple of hours later, he was right in my face smiling.

"Hey sleepy head!" He laughed and kissed my forehead. "You forget about our lunch date?"

"Sure did, but I'm getting up now!" I told him as I rose from the bed and listened to my stomach growl.

"Cool, I'll give you some space. I'll be in the living room waiting for you beautiful," Tay wooed making me blush like he always did.

When the door closed behind him, I couldn't stop wondering why I hadn't heard from Damarr. I mean, here Tay was popping up every day to make sure he saw me. Shit, Damarr hadn't dropped by one time!

Taking my cell off the charger, I saw that it was fully charged, and I had no missed calls. Seeing that Damarr wasn't reaching out, I started thinking it was because I ignored him the day before.

"Shit, a man who's gonna give up that easily, I don't need!" I huffed but still couldn't shake the attraction that I had for Damarr.

"Damn!"

Tay just had to come back to town at the wrong time and throw so much confusion into my life just when it started to become brighter with Damarr in it!

What was I going to do? As always, I had no clue.

Temporarily shaking the ill feelings off, I ran through the shower and came out smelling and looking great a half-hour later. The grin on Tay's face showed me that he was feeling the dress that I was wearing.

Just as he opened his mouth to compliment me, Katrice yelled and got my attention by turning up the news that was airing on her TV in the living room. "Some child got shot by his brother in the projects! Only eight and six years old! Damn!"

As I glanced closer, I watched the reporter as she waved the microphone in front of Demisha as she was being interviewed.

"I don't even know how it happened! Oh my God!" she cried as she stepped away from the microphone in tears. I could see her being comforted by someone, but the woman was inconsolable. My stomach dropped when I saw her face filled with tears.

"Was that Demisha?" Tay questioned as he walked into the room from the kitchen.

After we all watched the horrifying segment, I was nearly in tears. I needed to reach out to Damarr to see if the little boy was okay.

Running back to my room, I used the privacy to reach out to him at least five times. No answer either time!

Giving up, I sucked it up and went out to lunch with Tay. Too bad that I couldn't fully enjoy myself because my mind was on Damarr's family.

Of course, I didn't care for Demisha, but I wouldn't wish that type of tragedy on my worst enemy. That shit was a 'no-no'.

"You barely ate or said a word during lunch Cashay. You okay baby?" Tay questioned as he drove me home.

"Yea, I'm good," I lied and thought of a reason to get rid of him so that I could go by Damarr's and check on him. I was truly worried after hearing about his little cousin getting shot.

Hell, the news didn't even say if he was dead or alive.

Thinking the worst, I got back to the house and faked a headache just to get Tay to leave. Then it was time! I was going over to Damarr's!

Hopping in my car, I was able to make it there in about 35 minutes. I was so worried about him. I knew he and Demisha didn't always get along, but I knew he must be feeling some kind of way about her little boy. Hell, I didn't even like Demisha's ass, but I felt horrible for her. I would feel just as horrible for any mother who had to go through something like this with their child.

The news reporter didn't say much about how it happened. She just said that the six- year-old got his hands on a gun and shot his older brother who was only eight. How could parents be so irresponsible to keep a loaded firearm in reach of small children?

I would never understand no shit like that. This was a senseless accident that didn't need to happen. Why hadn't they done at better job at securing that damn gun?

Arriving at Damarr's place with a cloudy head, I spotted his car was in the driveway. I was glad because that meant he was here. I took a deep breath and exited the car and wondered how he would feel about me just dropping by without any warning.

I mean, I did just show up out of the blue. I did try calling but he didn't answer. I knew he probably felt like I ghosted him for the past couple of days, but that wasn't his fault. It was mine.

I had been so busy with Tay that I had completely forgotten about Damarr. Tay made me feel excited about my big ass. When he looked at me, he made me feel good. Damarr did that too, but it was different with Tay. Maybe it was because we had known each other since we were kids.

I didn't really know what it was, but I knew that I didn't have any regrets about spending time with him.

Clearing my mind and focusing on the matter at hand, I knocked on the door a couple of times and waited for him to open the door. When Damarr finally did pull it back, I couldn't read the expression on his face. I didn't know if he was happy to see me. I didn't know if he was distraught about his little cousin. I didn't know anything.

"What... what... what are you doing here?" he stuttered.

"I don't want you to think that I just dropped by unannounced. I tried calling first, but you didn't pick up."

"My phone didn't ring."

"I called you though," I said as I showed him my call log.

He walked over to the counter and checked his phone. "Dammit! The phone is off," he said.

"I told you that I called."

I watched as he powered on his phone. "Fuck!" he cussed angrily.

"What's wrong?" I asked.

"Nothing. What are you doing here?"

"I came by because I was worried about you..."

"Worried about me? You're the one who been ignoring me the past few days," he said.

"Yea, but I saw the news..."

"The news? What happened on the news?"

Clearly, he didn't know what the hell I was talking about, but how could he not know? How could he not know what segment of the news I was talking about?

Before I could question him about it, the bedroom door opened. "I didn't know you had company," I stuttered in surprise.

"Hello," the pretty woman wrapped in a towel greeted me with her hand out.

I turned my attention to Damarr. "Who is she?" I asked.

"She, uhm, me can speak for myself. I'm Chandra, Damarr's girlfriend..."

"She's not my girlfriend!"

"Oh, no? Well, he's been trippin' since I showed up, but we're gonna work through it," Chandra assured confidently.

"Ain't nothing to work through," Damarr blurted out with a frown.

"Well, we're expecting a baby, so I'd say we definitely have some things to work through," she said as she patted her belly.

Well damn! And here I was worried about him and how he was doing. Clearly, I did not need to worry because he had things covered on his end.

"So sorry I interrupted whatever it was y'all were doing. Good luck to the two of you," I said as I turned to leave. "Damarr, don't bother calling me ever again! And tell Demisha that I hope her little boy recovers!"

"What? Her little boy? What happened to Demisha's son?" he asked nervously.

"Go watch it on the news! Or better yet, call your family!" I said and stomped out of the house.

Now, I knew I had no right to be angry, but I was. I was mad as hell that he kept that from me and had me feeling so damn guilty about spending time with Tay. If he had a baby mama, he should've said that shit!

"The fucking nerve!"

I peeled out of his driveway and left him and whatever explanation he had behind in the dust!

To be continued...

Made in the USA
Columbia, SC
10 June 2021